Scholastic Children's Books,
Euston House, 24 Eversholt Street,
London, NW1 1DB, UK

RAIDERS AND RUINS

■SCHOLASTIC

A division of Scholastic Ltd
London ~ New York ~ Toronto ~ Sydney ~ Auckland
Mexico City ~ New Delhi ~ Hong Kong

Published in the UK by Scholastic Ltd, 2009

ISBN 978 1407 10347 1

Printed and bound by Bookmarque Ltd, Croydon, Surrey

2 4 6 8 10 9 7 5 3 1

Papers used by Scholastic Children's Books are made from wood grown in sustainable forests.

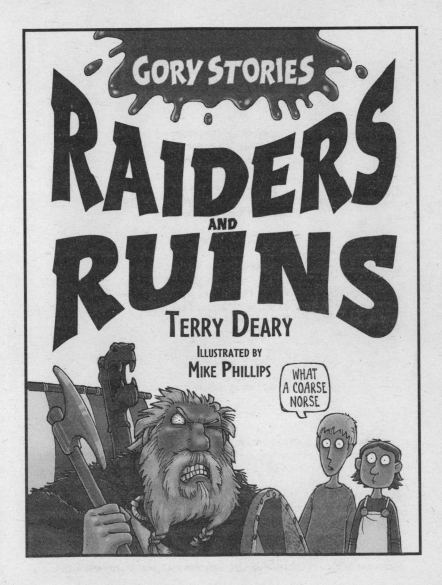

RAIN, A ROD AND A RACE

Father Patrick was a small man with eyes as wide and wild as the North Sea. He had the soft voice of an angel, yet every monk in Lindisfarne knew only a fool would ignore the wise words he uttered. His voice was gentle but his words scorched like molten gold.

'Not long now, my brothers,' he sighed and looked at the white sun in the clear sky. That sun shone through the narrow windows of the monastery church like rods of silver. Cups, crosses and candlesticks of gold and silver stood on the altar behind him. Their dazzling light behind his white fringe of hair looked like a halo.

'This is the way the world ends. The sun burns down and the crops curl up. The crops are like men who sin. They will shrivel in the heat of the racks of Hell.' He closed his bony hands and the monks shuffled their feet and felt sick at the thought.

Young Eric, the fair-haired novice monk, could feel his body shrivel, just the way Father Patrick said. The old man went on, 'And when the Earth is dry we will starve and die. And the Devil will take our wicked souls.' He raised his forefinger and pointed upwards. 'The sun is in Heaven and Heaven is sending it to burn the wicked.'

A warm wind blew into the chill, grey chapel and stirred up the dust that fifty pairs of sandals had trampled in.

Then the sun vanished.

A ragged black cloud had swooped across it like the

shadow of a hawk across the fields. There was a sudden
flash of purple light. Moments later there was a crash that
shook the chapel from its turf roof down to its stone floor.

Even Father Patrick looked surprised. The rain fell with a roar like waves on a pebbled beach, forcing its way through the roof and dripping into Father Patrick's eyes. Eric turned to young Ethelbert who was standing next to him. 'Looks as if Heaven has changed its mind,' he quipped.

Ethelbert twitched like a rabbit and hissed, 'Hush, Eric, Father Patrick will hear you.'

Too late. Father Patrick had already heard. His voice rose over the clatter of the rain. 'And the Lord sent thunder and hail, and the fire ran along upon the ground; and the Lord rained hail upon the land of Egypt!'

'Egypt?' Eric sniggered. 'Last time I looked we were in Northumbria. Still, at least we aren't going to shrivel like the crops and die.'

Father Patrick was not amused. He went on, 'God said, I will cause it to rain upon the Earth forty days and forty nights; and every living thing that I have made I will destroy from the face of the Earth.'

Eric shook his head. 'Better start building an Ark like Noah, ' he said and gave Ethelbert a nudge in the ribs.

Of course God gave Noah a bit of a warning before he sent the floods. Eric was a bit late to think of an Ark AFTER it started raining. He would drown before it was half finished. You could say he had Noah chance at all.

'I've never built a boat before,' Ethelbert whined.
'It was a joke, Ethelbert, a joke!' Eric sighed.

7

'Hee! Hee! Hee!' Ethelbert giggled. He stopped and he looked at Father Patrick but the old man was on his knees, praying. Water started to trickle through the door of the chapel and the monks crowded into the porch to watch the flood pour down from the leaden clouds.

'Thirty nine days and forty nights still to go, I reckon,' Eric said to cheer them all up.

Fifty monks stared upwards and watched sheets of blue light race across the sky and cracks of thunder shake the air.

The monk who kept the daily diary cried, 'Fiery dragons are flying across the world. It is a sign.'

'A sign of what?' Ethelbert asked, shivering.

'A sign of doom, of course!' the man answered.

'Doom?'

'Death and destruction.'

'It's just a thunderstorm,' Eric jeered. That was when he felt the hand grasp his shoulder. He turned and saw it was Father Patrick.

'You are the cleverest young novice we've ever had in this monastery. Yet sometimes you act like a demon sent to torment us. You have done since you arrived. You must learn it is wicked to mock the word of God!' Then he started muttering quickly. Eric knew the words because they came from the Bible he had been copying the week before. 'I will be his father, and he will be my son. When he does wrong, I will punish him with the rod of men.'

Scared that Father Patrick was about to give him a good hiding, Eric tore himself away from the monk's grip. 'You'll have to catch me first!' cried the disobedient boy and ran out into the storm.

Old Father Patrick turned to the monks. 'The tide is in. He cannot get off the island before nightfall. Catch him. Bring him to me. For his own good, we cannot let the Devil corrupt his soul.'

But Eric was not to be caught. He ran through the puddled paths and out of the monastery gates. He tumbled over the stony tracks and down to the eastern shore. The wind was coming from the west, whipping the North Sea waves like froth on a boiling pot.

He couldn't turn back. He headed towards the sea and his sandals sped over the turf of the cliff top. A tall monk with legs as thin as Father Patrick's rod was leaping over the rutted roads. In a race around the island the tall monk would catch Eric as soon as sneeze.

But Eric was not planning to race around the island. Eric knew exactly where he was going. He dropped over a shallow cliff just a few paces from the water's edge – a cliff no higher than a tall and leaping monk.

Who should arrive a bat-wing's beat later at the cliff edge? Yes, a tall and leaping monk! How did you guess? The tall monk, whose name was Brother Alcuin, stopped and skidded on the slimy seaweed. He looked at the lashing grey waves that crashed against the stony beach. His mouth fell open in a circle as round as the shaved spot on his head. He turned and looked back into the whistling wind.

Q: Why was the wind whistling? A: Because it didn't know the words to the song. (Oh, all right. That is a VERY old joke. But this is a very old story. Learn to live with it and stop complaining.)

'He's disappeared!' he called to the mass of monks who stood panting with Father Patrick.

The old monk reached the cliff edge and cried, 'Oh no! The Devil has swept his soul to Hell. If only he'd listened.'

'That may be,' the tall monk said, 'But if the Devil has his soul, where is his body?'

Father Patrick's thin hair whipped about in the wind. 'Washed out to sea, Brother Alcuin.'

'Oh, no! Poor Eric! My friend!' little Ethelbert cried.

Alcuin shook his head. 'He couldn't disappear that quickly. We'd see him floating.'

The monks squinted along the rain-lashed beach. Sea-worn rocks stood up among the pebbles, round and smooth from years of washing. They were humps of grey and black like Lindisfarne's slippery seals.

A flash of blue lit the scene and moments later a crash of thunder shook the crumbling cliffs. Monk clung to monk for comfort. They were all for heading back to the monastery to shelter from the bone-shaking blasts. But then Father Patrick pointed towards a shining black hump on the beach. 'It moved! God's teeth, it moved!'

'A miracle!' Brother Alcuin wailed.

'A coracle!' Father Patrick snapped back.

'A what?'

'Oh, Alcuin, you never leave the monastery garden. It is a coracle – a little fishing boat covered in leather and tar. Brothers leave them upside down on the beach till they need them. The boy is a fisherman – he knows all about coracles. He is hiding under that one! Get him – before any harm comes to him!'

Alcuin jumped down onto the pebbles. 'Ooooh! I've got pebbles in me sandals!' he groaned.

'Then take them off,' Father Patrick cried. 'Hurry!'

The coracle was shuffling down to the edge of the water like a turtle. The monks could see two small feet underneath.

As the icy waves lapped at his feet young Eric stood up and flipped over the coracle. It was light as a bird ... well, light as a very large, fat bird ... and it floated like a cork. The boy jumped in and pulled out a paddle that was wedged inside the round wooden frame.

'Run, Alcuin, run!' the monks urged as the tall brother tiptoed, barefoot, through the sharp shells and rough rocks crying, 'Ooooh! Me feet hurt!'

The wind caught the coracle and spun it round. While Eric struggled to push the little boat into the frothing sea, Alcuin stepped into the water. 'Ooooh! Me feet are freezing!' The talk monk stretched out a hand and gripped the edge of the little boat.

At that moment a fiery dragon of lightning appeared. It sizzled down from the low clouds in a ragged red rage. It snapped and sizzled at Alcuin's empty sandals and turned them into smoking soles and shredded straps. The lightning bounced across the beach and headed for the coracle.

When it struck, young Eric fell back inside the black boat and dropped the paddle into the sea. Alcuin screamed and staggered back onto the shore.

The west wind swept over Northumberland and ripped the reedy roofs off cottages and castles. Cows that failed to find shelter were blown through hedges and the wattle walls of humble houses.

Rain washed the bunnies from their burrows and swimming sheep struggled in new rivers that ran through their fields. Dogs ran into the rain and felt the water wash away their fleas while the fleas fled to the beds of hairy humans huddling indoors. 'God is angry,' Ethelbert sobbed as he struggled back to the safety of his cold, stone cell. 'Father Patrick was right. This is the end of the world! It's surely the end of Eric anyway.'

The west wind roared over the coast and tore at the towers of Lindisfarne Monastery. It pounced and bounced like a playful puppy towards the eastern shore of the island and snatched at the tiny coracle.

In moments the boy in his boat was swept miles out to sea on the torrent of the tide. Eric knew nothing of this. The lightning dragon's fiery flame had shaken the sense from his brain.

Night fell over the bobbing boat that, by some small

miracle stayed afloat.

Six monks carried Alcuin back to Lindisfarne and prayed over his singed, fringed head. He would live.

But what about Eric? No one could survive the raging North Sea in an open boat. Even if he woke, he was lost and far from shore. No paddle, no food, no fresh water.

No hope.

Looks like the end for Eric.

If you have tears, prepare to shed them now ... as the great poet William Shakespeare would have said ... if it hadn't been 800 years before he was born.

Well, that's the end of what was a very short story ... isn't it?

'What? Eric isn't dead YET!' you cry. No, but he's as good as, isn't he? What-what? You want to follow him all the way to his watery grave? May I say you are what they call a ghoul? Someone interested in death, disaster and horror. Oh, very well, if you insist ... ghoul.

A GIRL, GODS AND GUTS

Eric heard voices.

'He's dead,' a girl said.

The young monk struggled to open his eyes but the lids were caked with salt and wouldn't move.

'Is this Heaven then?' he wondered.

'Throw ... back ... sea,' a man said, struggling to speak English.

No. It wasn't Heaven, Eric thought. Maybe he was in Hell! This was his punishment. He had to drown, wake up, and be thrown back in the sea to drown again!

'The fish will eat him,' the girl sighed. She spoke in good English. 'What a waste.'

'The fish will eat him and grow fat,' the man said, but now he was speaking Norse. 'We will catch the fat fish and feast on them. Throw ... back ... sea,' he repeated in English to the girl.

'Don't!' Eric cried ... or tried to cry. His tongue was swollen like a pork sausage and it filled his mouth.

'He's alive!' the girl cried. 'Let me get a cloth and some fresh water.'

'Here, child,' a woman said. She spoke the Norse tongue like the man.

Eric felt cool, fresh water brush against his tongue and clear the salty plugs in his nose. He smelt fish and cattle. He felt like he was being rocked in a cradle and he felt a warm, salty breeze on his face.

The girl wiped his eyes. He opened them. The sun dazzled him and he closed them quickly. He squinted. The girl was leaning over him. She had dark hair chopped short and a round face turned brown by the sun.

'Is this Heaven?' he tried to ask.

The girl grunted, 'Uh?' and wiped his swollen tongue again. Eric moved his head a little. The man and woman were dressed in shabby woollen clothes. They were thin and their fair hair was going grey. The man bent and lifted Eric's head so he could sup water from the wooden spoon the woman was holding.

Eric tried to speak again. He squinted at the girl again. 'If you are an angel then how come you're so ugly?' he asked. Luckily the words tangled in his fat tongue and she didn't understand. He sat up and looked around.

'You're on a ship,' the girl explained. 'A knorr ... a trading ship.'

The rocking boat was almost as round as Eric's coracle but far larger. A soft breeze filled the sail of woven wool. The man walked to the back of the ship and grasped the steering paddle.

'How…' Eric croaked.

'I rescued you,' the girl said. 'We were caught in a storm and I was in the bows, looking out for rocks. Thorfinn almost ran you down. I rescued you,' she said and smiled happily. 'I am so-o glad you lived.'

'Thanks,' Eric whispered.

'I'm going to feed you and make you strong again,' the girl promised.

The young monk nodded. The old woman was pulling at ropes to move the sail and catch the wind. She spoke to her husband in their own tongue. 'We have hardly enough food to feed ourselves,' she snapped.

The girl said. 'You can share my food until you're well again. Thorfinn and Freydis are mean about food. I'll bring you some porridge now,' she said and crossed the rolling deck and climbed into the cow pen where she started to milk one of the five cows that chewed on thin hay.

Eric looked at the empty sea and felt the wind that was driving the knorr in front of it. 'That's a west wind,' he said.

'Speak Norse,' the woman said in her own language.

Eric's mother had been from over the North Sea so he spoke Norse as well as he did English. But the girl who had saved him … she had spoken English, hadn't she? He shook his muddled head.

'You are from Norway?'

'Yes.'

'And this wind is taking us there?'

'Yes. We traded furs for cattle in England,' the woman said. 'Now we are going home.'

'But it's not MY home.'

The woman shrugged her bony shoulders. 'You want to go back to England?'

'Yes.'

The woman stretched out a thin finger and pointed back into the wind. 'Then your little boat is on the deck. Off you go!'

'I can't see land ... I don't know which way to paddle!' Eric objected.

The woman threw back her head and showed some yellow teeth in a gap-toothed grin. 'Don't worry about that! You'll be swamped and drowned in the next storm that comes along. Go on ... kill yourself again. But Hilda won't be pleased.'

'Who's Hilda?'

The woman sighed. 'The English girl that saved you. Our slave. You owe her a life. You will have to pay her when we reach Norway.'

Eric sank back onto the deck, helpless and muttering, 'I don't want to go to Norway.'

The girl returned with some thin oatmeal in milk that was still warm from the cow. Eric swallowed it and it hurt his throat. But he felt his strength returning.

By the time the sun was low in the sky behind them he was able to help out on the ship. He took the steering paddle from the man, Thorfinn. 'You can sail?' the old man asked.

'It was my job back home ... before I joined the

17

monastery. My father owned a fishing boat on the River Wear – he taught me – and I was the fish-catcher for the monastery.'

Thorfinn nodded. 'Then you are valuable. Hilda did well to save you.'

'Did well?'

Thorfinn just nodded and went to work on a cattle pen that the cows had broken.

Eric slept in the shelter of a cabin on the deck. Thorfinn and his wife, Freydis, took turns at steering through the night. Hilda chattered till the young monk was exhausted.

'Where are you from?'

'Wearmouth on the river Wear,' he said.

'I'm from Jarrow on the Tyne, just eight miles from there!' she said. 'We don't like people from Wearside. Of course the land in Jarrow is poor. That's why my Mum sold me to the Norse.'

'Sold you!' Eric gasped. 'Your own mother sold you?'

Lots of parents would like to sell their children. I mean, your parents may not tell you that. But if someone came along with a good offer they would be tempted. Let's face it, when you were born they thought you were sweet. Then you grew up to be a Horrible Histories reader and they are shocked. So behave or you may just see an advert in the local paper: 'Child for Sale - going cheap to a good home' ... and it will be YOU.

'For three white bearskins. But I think I'm worth at least five, don't you?'

'She sold you, though. How cruel!'

Hilda shrugged. 'Better being a Norse slave than a starving free-born on Tyneside. She didn't think I was pretty enough to sell for marriage. Not that I'm ugly...'

Eric said nothing. 'I said "not that I'm ugly"...' she repeated.

'Oh, no ... just a bit plain maybe,' he said.

Eric did NOT know much about girls. Not many boys do – even if they live to be 100. So, boys, listen carefully and I will tell you one thing I do know ... if a girl tells you she is 'ugly' or 'plain' she WANTS YOU TO ARGUE WITH HER. Even if it's true about her ugliness ... especially if it's true. Eric didn't have me to tell him this. You have, so don't make his B-I-G mistake.

A spark of dragon-fire flashed in her eyes but Eric didn't see it. Hilda managed a tight smile. 'Anyway, your mother gave you to the monastery. Same thing!'

'No. No it's not!' Eric argued hotly. 'My father was a fisherman but he drowned at sea. She knew the monastery would care for me.'

Hilda sniffed. 'And she met another man, I suppose?'

'Yes ... but...'

'I thought so.'

Eric fought with his rage. 'I will learn to read and write and I could be as famous as Saint Bede. I will also end up going straight to Heaven when I die and standing on the right hand of God!'

Hilda snorted. 'Don't go spouting that nonsense in Norway! They believe in different gods there. Cruel gods. There is one god they call Loki – he upset the other gods so they slit open his stomach, pulled out his guts and used the guts to tie him to a tree!' The girl pulled a blanket over her and lay back sleepily. 'They may do that to you if you don't do as you're told. Goodnight...' she yawned. 'Sleep well.'

Eric decided he would return to Lindisfarne as soon as the next trading boat left Norway. He would take the beating from Father Patrick and settle down to become a good monk. That was why he had been saved from the sea. It was a sign from Heaven – a second chance. He muttered a prayer of thanks and turned over to sleep.

But Eric's sleep was disturbed by dreams of being tied to a tree with his own guts while Father Patrick beat him with a rod.

Still the nightmare wasn't as bad as what was really going to happen to him...

***

Eric woke and stretched. Hilda was already awake and eating a bowl of porridge that she shared with him. There were some clothes beside her and she patted them. 'Thorfinn made you a shirt and trousers while you slept,' she said.

'I have my robes,' Eric replied.

'They're no good in Norway. You need working clothes.

They don't like monks back in the village. They may even give you to the berserker to kill … for practice,' she sighed. 'That would be a waste.'

'What's a buzz-urkie?'

'Ber-serk-er,' she said as if she were talking to an idiot. 'I thought you spoke the Norse tongue.'

'My mother never taught me that word … it means "bear" and "shirt" but it doesn't make sense…'

'The Norse warriors go into battle with leather jerkins, helmets and shields so the arrows and swords can't hurt them. But the berserker goes into battle with a bearskin shirt and a wolf-skull on his head.'

'Is he mad?'

'Oh, yes! Daft as a three-legged dog. Our berserker is called Magnus – Mad Magnus. He practises by fighting bears and wolves … when he's really angry he wrestles with trees!'

'Do the trees ever win?' Eric jeered.

'I bet he wouldn't mind slitting you slowly into slices!' Hilda grinned. 'Berserkers just get themselves into a real rage and they think the gods will protect them … or kill them.'

Eric nodded. 'Yes … my mother told me that.' He frowned and tried to remember. 'She said I should never be afraid. The gods will decide when I am going to die – I could wear all the armour in the world but if I am doomed then I will die.'

'That's right. And if the gods want you to live then there's no point wearing armour. The gods didn't want you to drown yesterday … that's why they sent me along to save you!' she smiled.

Eric shook his head. 'The monks don't believe our God works like that! I'd get a beating if I said that to Father Patrick!'

'Only if the gods wanted you to get a beating,' Hilda shrugged. 'Now, change out of your robes and finish this porridge. I want you fit and strong when we go ashore.'

Eric felt a prickle of a tear in the corner of his eye. 'Thanks, Hilda. You are the kindest person I've ever met. An angel. Our Bible tells the story of the Good Samaritan – he rescued someone and cared for him because he had such a good heart.'

Hilda snatched up her blanket and made sure it covered her face as she folded it. After all, it would not do to let the boy see her choking back her laughter.

When she had calmed herself she looked at the boy seriously. 'The people from the River Tyne hate the people from the River Wear,' she said. 'We're born to be enemies.'

Eric climbed to his feet and gripped her by the shoulders. 'I know ... and the Samaritan was the enemy of the man he rescued! That's why it is so wonderful!'

She pulled herself free and ran to the front of the boat. So he couldn't see the tears of laughter running down her salt-stained cheeks.

Gulls clacked and wheeled over the mast. Eric knew that was a sign they were close to land. He was eager to land and find the next boat back to Lindisfarne. He pulled on the rough woollen shirt and trousers that Thorfinn had made. 'The tales I will have to tell Ethelbert when I get back,' he sighed.

Before the sun was very high in the sky he could see

mountains and rocky shores ahead. Hilda stood at the prow of the boat and called back, 'Can't you make this tub go any faster, Thorfinn?'

'What did she say?' the Norse asked Eric.

'She asked if you could go faster.'

'Huh,' the man grunted. 'I wish she could speak Norse better. She would be worth more.'

'Why is she in such a hurry?'

His wife, Freydis, cut in. 'The Thor's Day market starts at noon. She doesn't want to miss it.'

'To sell the cows?' Eric asked.

Freydis snorted. 'No. Hilda has something much more valuable to sell. Something worth two cows or more!'

'Treasure?' Eric gasped.

'Precious treasure,' Freydis nodded.

The thought excited Eric. He couldn't wait to reach the market. 'Can't you make this tub go any faster, Thorfinn?' he laughed.

Of course he was making a mistake. A big, fat, miserable mistake. But you knew that already, didn't you?

MAGNUS, MUD AND A MONSTER

Let me tie your hands behind your back,' Hilda said to Eric as the knorr nudged the wooden jetty.

'Why?'

'You are a stranger here. Someone may try to kill you,' she said sweetly. 'We don't want that, do we?'

'No, but how is tying my hands going to help?' the young monk cried.

'If they see you have been tied then they will think you belong to me – my slave. No Norse would harm another person's slave.'

As Thorfinn and Freydis drove the frightened cows down a gangplank onto the jetty, Hilda tied Eric's hands behind his back with a ship's rope. 'Do you have to tie it so tight?' he moaned.

'Oh, yes! We don't want this to look like some sort of trick,' Hilda told him.

'But it is a trick,' Eric muttered.

'Oh it's a trick all right!' Hilda laughed. 'Now let me tie a rope to each ankle. I'll leave just enough slack so you can shuffle along, but not enough for you to run.'

'There's nowhere to run to,' Eric said, looking over the village.

In front of him was a huddle of about fifty wooden huts with turf roofs. There was one much larger hall in the middle. The paths were damp and muddy and he guessed the floors inside the huts were just as bad. Mangy

24

dogs trotted round, sniffing for food scraps. Goats and pigs grazed in little pens for thin grass. They looked even more miserable than the people.

Behind the village there were some bare fields that had been cropped of their corn. Slaves were carrying bags of animal droppings and scattering them on the fields with their hands. Behind those fields the land rose steeply into a half-circle of mountains. Even the high passes between the mountains were thick with snow. It looked as if the only way in or out of the village was from the sea.

Outside the great hall there was a low wooden platform. A man was showing chickens to the crowd and they were calling out bids. The villagers were thin and weary. But one man stood at the side of the platform and he was twice the size of anyone else. His huge round face had folds of fat that almost hid his eyes. His mouth hung open and his beard was stained with food. Eric could smell him at ten paces.

'Who's that?' he whispered to Hilda.

'Mad Magnus, our village berserker,' she said.

'Why isn't he wrestling trees?' the boy asked.

'He only does that when he feels the urge to fight. He's too hungry these days ... like the rest of us. The crops were bad this year and even the fish seemed to swim away somewhere else.'

'Why doesn't he work for his food like the rest of us?'

'They say he is too clumsy,' Hilda shrugged. 'It'll be a hard winter.'

'Then the sooner I get back to Lindisfarne the better,' Eric muttered.

Hilda smiled a sweet, hollow smile. A man who stank of fish came up to her. His skin was like leather and the creases were stained white with salt from a life on the sea.

'What are you asking for this treasure?' he asked Hilda.

She frowned and said in broken Norse. 'Sorry – I do not understand?'

Eric thought it was time he helped his Samaritan angel. 'The man asked you what price you want for your treasure?'

'Thanks,' Hilda said. 'Tell Rollo it will go to the highest bidder.'

Eric repeated the message.

'What does it do?' the fish-scented man asked.

'It catches fish,' Hilda said.

The man called Rollo rubbed his hands. 'Perfect!'

'Perfect,' Eric repeated in English, then he asked Hilda, 'What's he talking about? What is this treasure?'

'You'll soon see.'

Thorfinn was selling his cattle on the platform and villagers were bidding with weapons and bags of corn, furniture and promises of enough wood to build a house.

When the last cow was sold and led away, Mad Magnus stepped forward. 'Any more?'

Hilda waved an excited hand, 'Yes, Magnus! Yes!'

Magnus frowned till his thick eyebrows met. 'Bring it forward!' he said. Hilda understood.

The girl jumped onto the platform and tugged at Eric's rope.

'You want MY help?' he smiled. 'With the words?'

'Something like that,' Hilda said.

'What am I bid?' Hilda cried.

'What is she bid?' Eric echoed.

'A cow!' someone called.

Hilda laughed. 'A cow! You are madder than Magnus if you think I would part with it for a cow!' she cried in English.

'You are ... erm ... mad as Magnus if you think she would sell it for a cow,' Eric told them.

The berserker stepped so close to Eric the boy was choked by the smell of rotten flesh – he guessed the bearskin hadn't been cleaned very well. 'Magnus not mad!' the berserker growled.

GET ON WITH IT!

'I didn't say you were!' Eric squeaked.

Magnus jabbed the boy with a finger as grey and flabby as a baby seal. 'Don't upset me. Magnus goes berserk if he gets upset. Magnus tears people to pieces. First he pulls off the arms and then the legs and then the head!'

Hilda sighed, 'Eric ... just tell him to push off and have a wash.'

Eric turned and said, 'Hilda says you should ... er ... she would very much like it if you would ... erm ... let her get on with selling her treasure.'

'Yeah?'

'Yes ... Magnus ... sir,' Eric said with a weak smile.

'Treasure not worth much with arms and legs ripped off,' Magnus muttered as he turned away.

'Eh?' Eric blinked. 'But...'

'One cow ... not enough,' Hilda said in bad Norse. She held up six fingers. 'Six cows!'

The crowd muttered among themselves and shook their heads. Then the fish-smelling Rollo stepped forward. A small boy stood beside him. A boy who was scrubbed cleaner than a polished pin. His leather jacket was covered with flower patterns, sewn on with silk and his shoes had warm wooden soles to keep him out of the mud. 'Buy it, Daddy!' the boy ordered.

'I will do my best, Harald,' the man said and patted the boy on his carefully combed hair. Rollo turned back to Hilda. 'Three sheep,' he said.

'Six sheep,' Hilda said.

'Four sheep ... not one sheep more.'

Hilda leaned towards him. 'It comes with its own little

fishing boat, Rollo. All you have to give it is a nice net and then sit back and watch the herring come home.'

The little boy stamped a shoe, 'You HAVE to have it, Daddy.'

Rollo nodded slowly. 'Six sheep it is!' he called out and the villagers began to cheer and clap.

Even painfully puzzled Eric gave a gentle clap. 'Well done, Hilda – you made a hard bargain. What were you selling?'

'A thrall,' the girl said and passed the rope to Rollo.

'But a thrall is the Norse word for slave. What slave?' Eric asked looking around.

'You,' Hilda said. 'I may be plain ... but it's better than being plain stupid, Eric.'

'You can't sell me!' he gasped as Rollo's son tugged on the rope. 'I'm a free man!'

Hilda shook her head a little sadly. 'No. You WERE a free man. But you threw away your life. You threw it into the sea. I gave it back to you, so your life belongs to me.'

'But ... stop it, boy!' Eric cried as the little boy yanked on the rope. 'But Hilda ... you were my Samaritan! The Samaritan in the Bible didn't SELL the man he'd rescued.'

'Aw! Really?' she smiled. 'He did in the Bible our priest read in church! I'll see you around I'm sure ... but I'll be a bit busy shearing my sheep and spinning warm winter wool to swap for food. Maybe it won't be such a hard winter after all!'

'I thought you were an angel!' Eric wailed.

'An angel from Hell,' she spat and her face turned

fierce. 'What I REALLY love is that you are one of those weird Wearsiders. Selling a miserable monk for six sheep would be fun ... but a wet Wearmouth wastrel is a joy. Now get off to Rollo's house before little Harald yanks your arms off.'

Now here's a strange thing ... more than a thousand years later, the people of Wearside and Tyneside are still not very fond of one another. The two rivers are still just eight miles apart but the people are more like a million miles apart. Times change quickly. Rivers, and people, change more slowly than a slug with a shortage of slime.

As Harald yanked the rope again the young monk cried out, 'No one can MAKE me be a thrall!'

Hilda spread her hands. 'No, but if you don't work, Rollo won't feed you. A master owns a thrall's life. He could kill you if he wanted. But that would be a waste so he may ask for his sheep back. If the sheep go back to Rollo then you go back to the sea where I found you ... but you will not have your little boat and your hands and feet will be tied. Bye!'

Eric's shoulders dropped in defeat and he let little Harald lead him to a cottage by the shore.

'There's a muddy puddle in the path,' the little boy said. 'Lift me up and carry me over it, thrall.'

Eric placed his filthy hands around Harald's clean neck and lifted him into the air. 'Awk!' the boy squawked. Eric dropped him carefully into the deepest part of the puddle. 'You will sleep in the hen house tonight for that, you pathetic plate of porridge!' Harald screamed.

And that's where Eric slept. And wept. He wanted nothing more than the cold hard bench in the grim grey cell back at Lindisfarne. Father Patrick's ruthless rod was better than this little Norse brat's bullying.

At least the hens gave Eric some eggs, and he swallowed them raw as he huddled in the straw for warmth. It was colder here than back in England. He lay back and looked up at the stars.

'If you are up there, God, would you like to help me get back home?'

God didn't reply.

'I'll pray six times a day and do good deeds among the poor people of Northumbria if you'll let me get home!'

God didn't do deals.

Eric sighed and thought of ugly Hilda. She had made a good enough life for herself ... even better now she'd sold a thrall for six sheep. Maybe life wouldn't be THAT bad, the boy thought.

'There are two things to look forward to,' he said to the stars. 'First, getting home and second … getting revenge.'

***

Eric rose cold and stiff when little Harald came and unfastened the hen house gate. The boy scattered corn on the ground for the hens and some struck Eric in the face. Then he turned and walked back into the house as if Eric wasn't even there.

Rollo came out of the house with a net and as Eric rose to meet him he snapped, 'Well, thrall, let's see how good you are at fishing, shall we?'

'I'm the best on the River Wear,' Eric replied.

'Pah! No one is better than me … that's why I am the village fisherman — but this year the fish are few.'

'Maybe you are looking in the wrong place,' Eric said.

Rollo curled back his thin upper lip. 'No one can look for fish … you sail out, you cast your net and you haul up all you can.'

'But there are some places better than others,' Eric said eagerly.

'I know that! I know that! I know!' Rollo raged.

'Fish move to where the food is. If you've been fishing in the same old places then of course you can't catch them.'

'Don't try to teach me my job!' the fisherman fumed like a furnace.

'Give me a week and I'll find them. I'll search north and south and bring home enough to feed the fattest faces in the village … even a face as fat as Mad Magnus's…'

'No!' Rollo said suddenly. 'No. You will sail north and

you can sail out to the west.' He lunged forward and gripped Eric by the arm till it hurt. 'But you must never … never ever go south into the next bay!'

'Why not?'

Rollo was breathing fast and his eyes were as wide and wild as Father Patrick's when he was preaching. 'Monsters.'

'Monsters?'

'A sea monster. A sea monster so big it would swallow you and your boat in one bite. If you ever go south to the next bay I will kill you, thrall, kill you!'

'If the monster doesn't kill me first?'

'Eh?'

'Well you can't kill me if the monster kills me first, can you?'

'Stop playing word games with me, boy. I'm talking about the Midgard Serpent – the child of Angrboða and the god Loki. You've heard the stories.'

'My mother told me some old tales,' Eric said. 'I never believed them! The monks say they are foolish.'

'We shall see who is foolish when you paddle back here without a head! Beware Jörmungandr, the Midgard Serpent … and stay away from South Bay!'

The Norse said Jörmungandr grew so large it stretched all the way around the world until it could swallow its tail. How sad is that? If you could stick part of your body in your mouth it may be your thumb or even your big toe. But would you stick your bottom in your mouth? I don't think so. Sometimes it is no fun being a monster.

Eric shook his head slowly as Rollo stomped away into the house. He picked up a hen and looked into its beady black eyes. 'First, I show them I am a fisherman, third, I get my revenge and fourth, I sail back home.'

'Cluck! Cluck! Cluck!' the hen cackled.

'Ah! You want to know what is second? Why, pay a visit to the Midgard Monster of course!'

STONES, SANDALS AND SOUTH BAY

Eric picked up his coracle. It was like meeting an old friend. He even spoke to it like a friend.

> This is quite normal. Even 1200 years after Eric's time, men are still talking to their cars as if they are friends. They talk to them the way mothers talk to babies. 'Let's get you washed, shall we?' What is very unusual is if the baby says, 'OK, that's fine by me. I do smell a bit.' What is even MORE unusual is if a car answers back.

'Pity we can't escape to Lindisfarne today,' he said. 'But when I do escape I'll not leave you behind. I promise.'

A stream ran through the village with a bridge across it made of three pine-tree trunks. Eric placed the coracle in the water by the bridge, climbed into it, and let it drift out into the sea. Where the stream met the sea there was a narrow strip of sand. Standing on the edge of the sand, arms folded and looking out to sea, stood Magnus the berserker. 'Go north,' the man grunted in a voice as rough as his bearskin shirt. 'You go south and Jörmungandr will swallow you.'

'He's too busy swallowing his tail,' Eric laughed.

Magnus didn't see the joke.

'You make fun of our gods and I will swallow you,' he roared.

Eric let the coracle drift past him. 'One day Thor will kill Jörmungandr,' Eric said, remembering the tales his mother had told him. 'Then he will drown in the monster's poison. Tasty, eh?'

Magnus looked out to sea and nodded. 'The day will be called Ragnarok – the last day of the World. One last great battle between the gods and the giants when everything will be destroyed. Those who fight bravely will join the gods in Valhalla...'

'Heaven.'

'And those who run will go to Hell.'

Eric shook his head. Father Patrick said it was the other way around! The peaceful would go to Heaven and the violent would end up in Hell. 'If I see Jörmungandr, I'll say hello from Magnus.'

Magnus's dark brows met in the middle of his nose. 'You will not go to South Bay. If you do and Jörmungandr doesn't kill you, then I will!'

Eric believed the berserker. He looked down into the coracle. 'So, first we have to get revenge on that girl ... last we have to escape back to Lindisfarne. But now there's something else we have to do isn't there?' The coracle didn't answer. 'We have to find out what is in South Bay!' the young monk whispered. 'But not today, my friend. Not today. For today we have to show these Norse folk how a Wearsider can catch fish!'

For a long while he left the paddle in the bottom of the boat. The coracle spun and danced on the waves and drifted with the currents. The net stayed in the bottom of the boat. 'Fish follow food,' Eric told his boat. 'Find the food and we find the fish.'

From time to time he dipped his hand into the water and brought some up in the palm of his hand. In the strong swelling sea the water was clear, but as he drifted towards the southern end of the bay it turned a pale green. 'Weed,' Eric smiled and remembered how his father had taught him to test the water like this. 'This is where we'll find our fish!'

He lowered the net and as the sun rose in the sky he fished till the coracle was full. He was now at the tip of the southern headland.

Round the corner was South Bay – the one he had been told to stay away from.

The water slapped against the leather sides of his little boat. But another sound drifted over the water. The clack of metal on metal and metal on wood. The sound was coming from the secret South Bay. 'Maybe they're making a new village. We'll have to have a look one day soon,' he said to the coracle.

As Eric raised his paddle to head back he heard a soft whoosh and a massive splash half-filled his boat with water. The slimy pile of fish at his feet started to gasp and writhe in the water. A large rock had been thrown from the cliff top. If it had hit the coracle it would have split the leather and scattered the wooden frame like driftwood.

Eric quickly paddled away from the foot of the cliff and scooped water out with his hands. When he looked up he saw a small boy standing at the edge of the cliff. The boy had a rock in his hands as large as his head and was waiting to throw it.

The young monk paddled along the edge of the cliff till he was out of reach then jumped into the shallow water on the rocky beach. He pulled the coracle and its catch of fish out of the water and ran across the beach. There were paths up to the cliff top made by the sheep that wandered there. If he raced fast enough he'd catch the stone-thrower before he escaped.

Loose stones skidded under his sandals as he gripped at tough bushes to pull himself upwards. At last he reached the soft, springy turf at the top of the cliff and ran towards the edge.

The boy had hardly moved. He had dropped the rock at his feet and stood with his arms folded across his chest. Eric breathed deeply and remembered Father Patrick preaching, 'Do not be angry, and turn away from rage; do not worry – it leads only to evil.'

He calmed himself and looked at the boy. It was little Harald, the son of Rollo the fisherman. The boy gave a sly smirk. 'You can't touch me, thrall. My father will have you beaten to death.'

'You could have killed me, you stupid, spoilt, little worm,' Eric said quietly.

'I know,' Harald said happily. 'But Daddy told me to!'

Eric blinked. 'Your father told you to kill me?'

'Daddy said I had to watch you. He said that if you went too near South Bay I had to stop you.' Suddenly the boy leaned forward and put out a tongue. 'Yahhhh! I threw the rock to warn you, thrall-monk. If I'd wanted to hit your pathetic little boat I could have done.' He pointed to the rock by his feet. 'And if you'd gone another paddle-stroke closer I would have done! You are a thrall. Your life is mine to give or take. I don't care which.'

Eric stepped forward. 'Rollo should not send children to do a man's job,' he said softly. 'After all, a silly little boy could easily slip over the edge of the cliff and smash his empty little head against the rocks below.'

Eric took another step forward till he was just two paces from the hateful Harald. He expected the boy to back away to the edge of the cliff. But Harald stood firm.

'If I fell then the whole village would torture you like the great God Odin and tear out your eye!'

Eric told him, 'Odin gave up his eye – he swapped it for wisdom.'

'Well ... well ... well, you'll be swapping your eye for pushing me over the cliff.'

Eric grinned and took another pace forward, 'Oh, but it would be worth it, hideous Harald! It would be worth it.'

Harald put out his tongue even further and blew hard. 'Thrall-monk. Well you won't get to push me over the cliff because Mad Magnus will stop you!'

'Magnus was down at the village bridge last time I saw him,' Eric shrugged. 'No one will see you fall. I'll tell your father I saw you slip.'

'Aha!' you cry, 'Eric is not a good monk at all! He is going to murder poor little Harald and then tell lies about it. Aha! Aha!' In fact he is a liar – he is lying to scare Harald. He doesn't mean to kill him. 'Aha!' You cry again ... 'He is a bully!' Aha! I cry, you could be right. But it's better than being a murderer. Now can we all stop crying 'Aha!' Thank you.

'Magnus will tell him the truth, won't you Magnus?' the little boy giggled.

'Yes,' came the rumbling voice of the berserker from behind Eric.

Eric turned and smiled. 'Just having a little joke with my favourite friend!'

Magnus glared and drew his wide, rust-stained sword ... at least Eric hoped it was rust and not blood. 'Rollo told you to stay away from South Bay ... Magnus told you to stay away.'

'I told you so! I told you so! Pttthhhht!' Harald cried, sticking out his tongue. 'Give him the blood eagle, Magnus. I've always wanted to see the blood eagle.'

Magnus nodded. 'That is special. Only for great men, not for little monks.'

'Awwww!' Harald howled. 'I want to see the blood eagle! I want to! I want to!'

Eric shook his head and looked at Magnus. 'What is this bawling brat talking about?'

Magnus slid his sword back into its sheath and gave a crooked smile under his crusty beard. 'I'm glad you asked me that, thrall.'

'Are you?'

'Oh, yes! People think that because I'm big and brutal, I am stupid!'

'I can't believe that,' Eric said carefully.

'Oh, they do! Mad Magnus, they call me.'

'I'm shocked,' the young monk said.

'But I know all the old stories about the gods AND the stories about our Norse heroes!'

Magnus lumbered over to a rock and sat down heavily on it.

'Tell him about the blood eagle, Magnus!' little Harald squealed.

'Now the blood eagle is NOT a story of the gods...'

'Like Odin having his eye ripped out?' Eric put in.

'That's right. The blood eagle is something we Vikings do to our favourite enemies.'

'What's a Viking?' Eric asked.

Magnus shook his shaggy head. 'The people who live in the villages and the farms are the Norse people. But some of us only farm in the summer ... I mean we sow the seed and cut the corn and all that. But at other times we go out robbing people ... attacking other villages down the coast and stealing their cattle and sheep. We call that going a-Viking.'

'So-o,' Eric said, 'Vikings are Norse robbers. Pirates?'

'Warriors,' Magnus said sharply. 'Norse warriors.'

'Sorry, Norse warriors.'

'Well, the gods have been cruel for the last few summers and we can't live from farming any longer. We need to fight to live.'

'Ohhh! Tell him about the blood eagle!' Harald wailed.

'I was coming to that … now then, usually we attack a village and pillage it.'

'Pillage a village?' Eric asked as he moved to sit next to the giant Norseman.

'That means rob it and burn it down,' Magnus said. 'We kill the people if they try to stop us and we turn them into thralls if they don't. Of course we don't like killing them. I mean a thrall is useful, isn't it?'

'I suppose so,' the young monk nodded.

'Now, from time to time our warriors attack villages that have their own warriors and we have a really good fight. There's blood all over the beaches!'

'Sounds like fun,' Eric sighed.

'If there is one really, really great fighter then we may capture him alive. Then we don't kill him quickly. Oh, no, he deserves to die really slowly to show how brave he is!'

'Nice,' Eric said.

'They give him the blood eagle,' Harald chirped.

'We ties the hero to a tree … facing the tree, like,' Magnus went on. 'Then we uses our knives to snip his ribs away from his backbone.'

'That'll hurt,' Eric gasped.

'That's the idea. Of course, it doesn't kill him!' Magnus chuckled. 'We pulls the ribs out, reaches inside his back and grabs hold of his lungs and pulls them out. That doesn't hurt at all!'

'Why not?'

'Because it kills him doesn't it? Cor! They calls me stupid. Just imagine if I rips your lungs out thrall-boy! Cor! You wouldn't be alive after that! We spread the lungs over the back like the wings of an eagle – that's why we calls it the blood eagle.'

'Show him, Magnus! Do it to him!' Harald screeched.

'No, no! I'm too clumsy! Anyway, the thrall-monk's not a great hero!' Magnus told him. 'No! We'll probably just pluck his eyes out if he ever goes round into South Bay!'

He stood up and ruffled the hair on top of Eric's head with a horny hand.

'How did he do that?' you ask, trying to catch me out. 'Eric's a monk and monks take the hair off the top of their head – they rub it off with a rough stone, don't they?' 'Well,' I answer, 'that's because Eric was a "novice" – still just training. He wouldn't get to scrub his head till he was a proper monk.' You want to catch me out? You'll have to try harder than that!

'Have a good day's fishing, boy.'

'Thanks,' Eric said weakly.

'Awwww! I wanted to see his lungs ripped out!' Harald sighed.

FISH, FILLETS AND FOWL

When Eric returned to the village Rollo was startled. 'Fish! Where did you get all that fish?' The young monk took a stick and scratched a simple map in the mud at the edge of the stream. 'Here is the village in the bay,' he said drawing a 'C' shape to show the coast. 'The sea current meets the stream here and washes the water clean...' He made a cross in the centre. 'The weed is pushed to the south edge of this bay and that's where to find the fish. In the shallow water.'

'My boat's too big to go there,' Rollo grumbled.

'That's why we use coracles in England,' Eric told him. 'Now I guess the next bay to the south is even richer in fish. If you let me go there then I would make you the richest man in Norway!'

'No!' Rollo croaked. 'The Midgard Monster will get you. I paid six sheep for you and I don't want to lose you before your fishing has paid me back!'

The novice nodded. 'Tell that to Harald,' he muttered.

'My son will grow up to be one of the greatest heroes in Norway!' Rollo cried. 'He is wise for his age. People respect him. Even adults obey him.'

'And if they don't he stamps his foot and pokes his tongue out at them.'

'Yes ... no!' Rollo waved a warning finger. 'Don't upset my Harald.'

'No, Rollo.'

'Now here's a gutting knife. Get started filleting this fish. We'll sell half fresh today and keep half in salt to sell over the winter when the villagers are really starving.' Rollo rubbed his rough hands. 'They'll pay anything when they are starving. In winter, cod is king! Now get started.'

Eric took the knife and rubbed it on a stone till it was sharper than a bird's beak. He sliced down the belly of a fish, pulled out the guts and threw them into the stream. Gulls started to gather and scream as they fought over them.

Eric was halfway through the heap when he saw the girl race over the pine bridge and throw herself down beside him, gasping for breath.

'Hello, Hilda,' Eric said sweetly and waved the knife under her nose. 'Just wait till I've finished this fish then I'll fillet you next.'

'But I saved your life,' she panted.

'You saved my life so you could sell me as a slave, you witch!' His face turned red. 'Father Patrick told us the Bible says we must not allow a witch to live!'

'Well Father Patrick won't be saying it much more if I get my hands on him,' she spat. 'He sounds like a miserable, old woman-hater. All you monks are the same!'

Eric sighed. 'The smell of the fish is bad enough. The smell of a witch is worse. Leave me alone and go and play with your sheep.'

'I need to tell you something,' Hilda moaned. 'Will you listen?'

'Yes! You need to tell me you're sorry for what you did. You need to tell me you'll find a way to get me back to Lindisfarne. Or maybe you need to tell me you have some dreadful disease and you'll die today. Then I'll say hooray!'

'The Norse are having a meeting. The warriors and the elders of the town. They are meeting in the great hall at sunset,' she said.

Eric frowned. 'There are no warriors in the village,' he said. 'I've only seen farmers, fishermen and their wives.'

'Because the warriors are away somewhere. Plotting. They were talking about "Viking". But I don't know their tongue very well. What does Viking mean? You have to tell me!'

Eric jabbed the knife into a fish and ripped at it roughly. 'Viking means robbing. The warriors ... wherever they

46

are … sail down the coast and attack other villages, like pirates. The food is so short here they need to steal from other Norse people.'

Hilda picked up a headless herring and looked at it. 'But the other villages must have little left to steal.'

'I suppose that's right. And some of them have their own warriors … they put up a fight and drive the Vikings away. Even Magnus can't win every battle.'

Hilda threw the herring in a basket and wrinkled her plain face in thought. 'So they need to find new places to attack.'

Eric nodded slowly. 'That makes sense.'

'Places like England,' she said.

'No. It's too far. English towns aren't little farming villages like this. They have walls and fortresses and fighting men … you'd need hundreds of Vikings. The knorrs are just too slow and too small. England is safe.'

'In the meeting there was one word I understood,' Hilda said quietly. Rollo was walking down the path by the stream to collect the clean fish. Little Harald hurried by his side. Eric sliced quickly and Hilda spoke quicker. 'It was the word "monks".'

Eric's knife jerked with the shock. The razor edge missed his thumb by the thickness of a seal's whisker and tore at his shirtsleeve. 'Monks? But why…'

'Ah! Slave-boy, chatting when you should be working, eh?' Rollo cried. He brought down his stick sharply on Eric's shoulders.

'Well done, Daddy!' the horrible Harald cried. 'Do it again! Beat him till he bleeds! Then rip his lungs out.'

'Not until he's earned me my six sheep, Son!' Rollo said.

As he swooped and picked up the basket of gutted fish, seagulls scattered and soared. He threw the stick to Harald and used his free hand to grasp Eric's collar and drag him to his feet.

'Meet me back here at sunset!' Hilda cried after him in English.

'What did the ugly girl say?' Rollo asked.

'She said she hoped you'd feed me well for my day's work!' Eric lied.

'How many fish have you gutted?'

'Fifty at least.'

'Then you have fifty lots of fish guts to eat!' Rollo laughed.

'I threw them to the gulls.'

'Then you threw your supper away, thrall-boy. Now get in the hen house and stay there.'

The young monk was thrown into the wooden pen and the gate was barred behind him. He looked back through the bars and Harald was standing there poking out his tongue.

Eric sank back among the feathers and the bird droppings. The breeze off the sea was colder now. Winter was back. If storms lashed the coast he'd be soaked and catch a fever. He'd die. That would teach Rollo a lesson.

There was just one egg to eat and he supped some water from the leather bucket the hens drank from. Night fell and the wind grew colder. The wind carried the sound of shouting and then singing and clapping.

Inside the great hall Norse men were gathered to eat and drink.

But they were short of food. There wasn't enough for feasting. Who would get the best food? Some lord? No, there were a lot of men making that noise. Not the miserable men of the village.

Slowly it came to Eric.

Warriors.

Only warriors could have earned the right to the best food and ale.

But he'd only seen one warrior – Magnus the Berserker. A hen sat on Eric's lap and he stroked it. 'Remember what Magnus said?'

Cluck?

'"They won't even let me share the work" … that's what he said. He's too clumsy.'

Cluck!

'Where have this army of men been all day? Working?'

Cluck!

'Working at what?'

Cluck! Cluck! Cluck!

'No. I don't know what they're working at either … but we both know where they're working, don't we?'

'In South Bay.'

Eric almost swallowed his tongue when he gulped. 'A talking chicken?'

'No,' came a voice from the darkness outside the pen. 'A talking Tyneside girl.'

'Hilda?'

'I waited for you by the bridge. You didn't come,' she complained.

'Maybe because I'm locked in here, eh?'

He heard the bar being pulled back and the door creaked open on its leather hinges.

'Let's go,' she said.

'Where to?'

'Oh God's kneecaps, do I have to do the thinking for both of us?' the girl snapped.

'We need to work out what they're up to,' she said as she took his hand and led him round the side of Rollo's house. They slipped down the only street of the village towards the path that led south.

The noise from the great hall swelled louder then stopped suddenly, as if the visitors inside were holding their breath.

Hilda snatched at the boy's arm and dragged him towards the hall. A tall man stood in the light of a lantern and guarded the door. 'What do you want?'

'I'm master Thorfinn's thrall,' Hilda said quickly. 'He wants to see me.'

The Norse man drew his sword. 'He wants to see you in how many pieces?' he asked.

'But...'

'This is a meeting for the Vikings,' he said. 'Thorfinn is in there as an elder. He is speaking now. I will send him out when he is finished! If Sigurd will let him go.'

'Who's Sigurd?' Eric asked.

The guard pointed through the doorway to a tall young man with golden hair. He was stood on a platform

50

at the end of the hall and was speaking to the men inside. 'Sigurd is the Viking leader, of course. A warrior as great as Thor himself. There's your master Thorfinn getting up to speak now. So clear off. When he's finished I'll tell him you need to see him.'

'It doesn't matter,' Hilda sighed and dragged Eric to the side of the building. A large window had its shutter held open to let out the smoke of the flaming torches and the steam of the boiling pork. It also let out the stench of two hundred men. The two English spies looked in.

'What are they saying?' the girl asked.

'It's Thorfinn speaking … he says he's been across to England and seen the riches there … but they are well guarded…'

'We know that,' Hilda sniffed.

'But … wait … there are places the English call monasteries … full of feeble old men and children … they have treasures of gold and silver just waiting to be taken.'

'Cowards,' the girl hissed.

Eric nodded. 'It's not the way to get into Valhalla … attacking helpless, unarmed monks! Wait…'

'What's he saying?'

'When the time is right then he will lead them to the fattest ox in the herd.'

There was a massive cheer from the men in the hall and the men started singing and drinking again. 'The fattest ox? He's going to rob a farm?'

'No, no!' Eric said softly. 'The monasteries are like cattle waiting to be killed. Thorfinn will lead them to the richest one.'

'But there are a hundred monasteries. Which one does he mean?'

'It will be on the north-east coast of England … the easiest for them to reach. My home in Wearmouth is rich,' the boy said.

'I think not!' Hilda mocked and her voice rose dangerously. 'Everyone knows Tyneside has the greatest monastery the world has ever seen at Jarrow!'

'I think not…' Eric scoffed. 'Even Lindisfarne is richer than Jarrow.'

'Oh really? And have you ever been to Jarrow, you know-it-all novice?'

'No, but … but have you ever been to Lindisfarne?'

'Not inside, but, hey! If you are a sample of the sort of sheep-brained sops they have there I don't need to see inside the place.'

'Shut up!'

'Don't you dare tell me to shut up, sheep-brain!'

'No! I mean … I mean it doesn't matter if they want to attack Wearmouth or Jarrow or Lindisfarne, we can't do anything to stop them!'

'We can warn them.'

'How? Swim across the North Sea?' Eric cried.

Hilda fell silent at the thought. 'Sorry.'

'What?'

'It's no good us arguing. We need to find out as much as we can about the plan first…'

'I agree.'

'And then find a way to warn England.'

'I agree.'

'Easy.'

Cluck!

'I think your friend has followed you.'

SIGURD, SHIPS AND SWORDS

Eric and Hilda hurried back down the dark paths to Rollo's hen house. The boy had to be locked in again. Until they had a plan they had to stay out of trouble and go about their work as normal.

Hilda spoke quickly. 'Sigurd and the Vikings have a plan to attack a monastery in England ... but we don't know how they'll do it or which monastery. And of course we don't have any idea how we can escape to warn the English – even if we knew where they plan to attack.'

'No,' the boy agreed. 'But we know it has something to do with South Bay.'

'So, first, you have to see what they are up to in the bay.'

'Me?'

'Yes. They will have a guard on the path over the headland. I can't just walk over and say, "Good morning. What are you up to? Me and a skinny monk plan to stop you!" No. The only way to get there is in your coracle,' the girl told him.

'But little Harald watches that ... and he has Mad Magnus to help if he needs him,' Eric moaned.

'Then I will find a way to get rid of Harald,' Hilda said.

'Push him off the cliff?' the young monk asked hopefully.

'No! That will just cause more trouble. I have a way.

Leave him to me. Tomorrow you go fishing just as you did today. As soon as Harald leaves his lookout post you paddle round and see what you can see. I'll come back here tomorrow night and find out what you've learned.'

'If they don't catch me and give me the blood eagle,' Eric muttered.

'We have to take risks,' Hilda told him.

'I'll remember the risk YOU are taking as they rip my lungs out.'

'Oh, stop complaining,' she snorted. 'You have the heart of a hen!'

Cluck!

***

Winter winds were whistling over the North Sea and Harald was shivering in the weak morning sun. He watched as the thrall-boy Eric dragged his net in the waters below and filled his coracle with cod.

'Hello Harald!' a girl said. Harald had seen her in the village. She was the thrall of Thorfinn the trader.

'Hello ugly girl,' he said.

Harald spoke little English, Hilda spoke little Norse. They used simple words, a lot of hand-waving and drawing pictures in the mud with a wiggling stick. It would take a l-o-n-g time to give you every word, wave and wiggle. So I will give you what they MEANT to say. I am kind like that.

'Hello, handsome young man. You look like a Norse god, standing on this cliff top, facing the wild west wind. So handsome like a hero. Harald the Hero ... that's what they should call you!'

The round face of Harald looked pleased. 'It's true,' he said smugly.

'But even Thor had a terrible enemy, didn't he?'

'Well ... he had lots of enemies,' Harald said. 'My favourite is Utgarda-Loki – he said Thor couldn't sup a drinking horn dry. And Thor couldn't. That's because the horn was connected to the oceans of the world!'

'No, not Utgarda-Loki ... I was thinking of the Frost Giants.'

'Ah, yes. The Frost Giants of Niflheim ... the land of Mist and Ice.'

'I suppose you must feel like Thor in Niflheim sometimes? Stuck up here when the winds blow off the North Sea?'

Harald nodded and blew on his hands. 'I do.'

'Of course Thor was saved by the giant girl called Grid, wasn't he?' Hilda asked.

'Yes. She gave Thor a magical belt and some iron gloves.'

'Oh, but that's what YOU need, Harald! A maiden to give you some nice gloves ... and a warm cloak with a hood to wear over your fine coat!'

'I do. I wish Grid would help me,' he sighed.

'But you have me instead!' Hilda cried.

'You?'

'Yes. I have six fine sheep. I got them for selling the thrall-monk to your father at the market,' she said.

'I know, I was there.'

'I've been taking their wool and spinning it. Now I have enough to weave it into a fine cloak.'

'And gloves?'

'And lovely warm woollen gloves. A hero like you deserves them.'

'I do,' Harald agreed. 'Bring them to me now with a bowl of hot soup.'

Hilda pulled a face. 'Sorry, but I need to make sure it's a snug fit. If I make the cloak too small then the wind will slice through the gaps – too large and you won't be able to walk! Come with me to my hut at the back of Thorfinn's house. I will cut it and sew it to fit just right.'

Harald stuck out a bottom lip in a pout like a spout. 'I have to stay here. I have to make sure the thrall-boy doesn't paddle round into the next bay.'

Hilda stroked her chin. 'I have an idea ... there is a pile of stones at the edge of the cliff,' she said.

'Yes, I put them there ready. I'll throw them at the thrall's boat if he goes too far!'

'Ohhhh! You really ARE like mighty Thor – he threw thunderbolts! And he threw his mighty hammer. It was magical. The hammer always came back to him.'

Imagine it. A hammer that works like a boomerang. How useful is that? If a builder is putting tiles on a roof, and he drops his hammer, it will zoom back up to him. It will save people underneath having crushed skulls and save him having to climb all the way down to get it back. This is such a great idea I think you should go off and invent it. I'd do it myself but I have a story to finish writing...

'Yes,' Harald said. 'I am like Thor – but the rocks I throw don't come back to me. I'm sure I could make them if I wanted to!'

'I'm sure you could,' Hilda giggled in a girlishly gleeful way. 'But I thought you could take off your beautiful embroidered coat and hang it on the pile of rocks. When the thrall-boy looks up he will see the coat and think you are still on guard!'

Harald nodded. 'That's a very clever idea ... for a thrall-girl!'

Hilda made a tight fist of her right hand and wanted to punch Harald's pompous mouth. Instead she said softly, 'Thank you, sir.'

Harald slipped off his coat and hung it over the rock pile. Hilda lifted another rock and placed it on the collar to hold the flapping coat in place. From a distance it looked like a boy on guard.

Well ... it looked like a boy on guard if you were a man on a flying horse with one eye and half a brain ... on a foggy night ... in a snowstorm. And you are not a man with one eye on a flying horse, on a foggy night in a snowstorm, are you? Well? Are you? Oh, and by the way, if you say 'No' to that question I guess you agree with the bit that says you have half a brain! Heh! Heh!

Harald shivered and Hilda wrapped an arm around his shoulders as she led the way back to the village. With her free hand she waved madly to her partner in the coracle below. Eric waved back.

As soon as the cliffs were clear he began to paddle out to sea.

Grey waves rocked the boat and sea-spray chilled the young monk like the mists of Niflheim. He paddled into the wind and against the tide. The paddling warmed him up.

Eric reached the edge of the headland, looked back to see that no one was watching and paddled hard towards South Bay.

That was when he was almost swallowed by a dragon.

***

The dragon towered over Eric, taller than two men and rushing towards him. Its fierce eyes stared out to sea and its red snout opened wide to show sharp white teeth.

The head was held high by a neck of green scales and the neck was fastened to the front of a ship. Luckily it was a carved and painted wooden dragon.

But it was a sort of ship Eric had never seen in all his years in Wearmouth. He had seen a hundred knorrs — some were large enough to carry cattle and corn and some small enough to ferry people across the river. But they were all about as round as his coracle.

This ship with the dragon's head was slim as a snake and long as the great hall in the village. A dozen warriors were rowing it out towards the sea. Luckily they had their backs to Eric and he was able to scrabble with his paddle out of their way. He moved quickly towards the side of the headland and jumped onto the rocky beach. He tipped the fish onto the shore, turned the coracle over and crept under it. The coracle looked like a black rock, just as it had when he ran away at Lindisfarne and hid on the shore.

He lifted the edge of the coracle and looked out. The warriors were too busy to notice him so he was able to watch the dragon ship as it sped past him.

On the shore of the bay he saw the great Viking secret … there was a line of nine more dragon boats like this one. Some were finished and some were still being built. Wooden mallets struck chisels. 'I should have known that noise,' the boy muttered to his coracle. 'Ship builders at work. I should have guessed.'

He looked out to sea and saw the dragon boat that had almost run him down. It was turning in a wide arc. The warriors were pulling in their oars now.

A tall man with blonde hair heaved on a rope and a woollen sail rose on the mast. It was Sigurd, the warrior leader. The west wind caught the sail and it billowed like the throat of a croaking frog.

The men gave a cheer and stood up. Each man slipped a shield off the side of the ship and pulled a sword from his belt. The men beat their swords against the shields and made a fearsome noise.

They were being blown back towards the shore and the other ships. There was now no need to row.

The noise of the men was met by screams from the shore. The warriors on the shore had picked up shields and swords and were standing at the water's edge waiting to drive back the attackers.

Eric threw aside the coracle. No one would notice a boy at the foot of the cliffs. 'They are attacking their own men!' he gasped. 'What are they doing?'

The coracle didn't answer. It never did. The defenders were two hundred paces away from Eric but one figure stood out. A man with a shaggy, bearskin coat who waved a sword and screamed more wildly than the wolf-skull on his head had ever screamed when it was alive.

Magnus the Mad Berserker was worked up into a rage. His mouth was wide as a sea cave and no one went near him for fear of his swiping sword. His hairy shirt hung open and showed his hairy chest. He was the only man who didn't carry a shield. The gods would shield him if it was not his turn to die.

When the longship was twenty paces from the shore Sigurd pulled on a rope and the woollen sail dropped down the mast. The speed of the ship was enough to carry it crunching onto the stony shingle.

The men on the boat jumped into the icy water that came up to their knees and struggled through the sea to the shore. The defenders waited.

No attacker went near the raging wolf that was Mad Magnus. They stopped and faced one another.

At last the blond-haired Sigurd gripped the dragon neck and swung himself down from the ship into the shallow water. It was Sigurd who turned and boldly faced the berserker.

Everything went quiet for the beat of a seagull's wing. Sigurd barked an order and the attackers stepped forward to meet the men on the shore.

Mad Magnus roared and leapt at Sigurd. The two lines met.

Eric held his breath and waited for the clash of iron sword on iron sword.

Instead he heard the sound of…

A MADMAN, A MUSH AND A MAIDEN

Eric stood by his coracle and heard the sound of wood on wood.

And laughter. Lots of laughter.

Warrior attackers met warrior defenders and beat at one another with their wooden swords. If a man was struck with a sword he gave a great, gurgling cry and fell to the beach as if he was losing his life's blood.

Slowly the truth came to Eric's baffled brain. He had fought like that when he was a child back in Wearmouth. The English children called it 'play-fighting'.

The Viking warriors probably called it 'war practice'.

They were testing their new weapons – not wooden swords but wooden ships. A new way of fighting. Race up to a beach, leap ashore and strike before the enemy had a chance to stop them.

Across the sea the English guards would have a short time to see the fleet of ships, run to the village and the fields, let workers gather weapons and race to the shore.

It was speed that mattered. If the Vikings could race onto English beaches in their swift ships they could be robbing and killing before the villagers could say, 'Excuse me ... who are you then?'

It made the boy angry. 'It's cheating!' he moaned to his coracle. 'I know they're hungry but they could trade for food. They don't have to raid for it.' He kicked at a stone.

'We shall fight them on the beaches, we shall fight on the landing grounds, we shall fight in the fields and in the streets...' then he stopped. 'No we won't ... because they'll be attacking monks. There'll be no fighting – just plain massacre. And I'm the only one to save them!'

The rowdy fighting was dying down on the Norwegian beach and a new sound was coming along the shore to Eric's ears. The sound of worried cries.

The 'dying' men were on their feet and making a half circle around the only two warriors still fighting ... Sigurd and Mad Magnus.

Magnus was lost in a mist of murderous madness and screaming at the Viking chief. One warrior tried to grab hold of the berserker's arm but the wooden sword smashed against his helmet and knocked him down.

The sword was broken but that made it more dangerous. A dagger-shaped splinter was in the berserker's hand. It was too small for Sigurd to beat away with his own wooden sword.

Sigurd's sword cracked against the wrist of Magnus and that just made the monstrous man even angrier. With a wolf-howl he jumped forward and stabbed at Sigurd.

His leather jacket should have turned away the splinter but the broken blade slid in just below the belt and into the belly of the warrior chief.

Magnus pulled back the blade and looked at it. Eric was too far away but he knew it would be bloody. The scent of blood seemed to make Magnus wild as a dog with piece of raw beef. He began lashing out at the warriors as they moved in to help their fallen leader.

The berserker's voice carried over the slapping waves to Eric. 'The gods have said I will live – no one can hurt me! No one! No … ouch!'

Why did the mighty warrior cry 'ouch'? Because one of the attackers had run back to the boat and dragged an oar back with him. As Magnus faced the sea the warrior swung the oar behind the mad man and crashed it into his skull. The oar split, the berserker stood dazed, then he fell forward like a mighty pine tree.

The warriors hurried to gather up Sigurd and Magnus and carry them back along the path to the village. It was time for Eric to hurry back too. He collected the fish he'd spilled on the beach and threw them back into the coracle. Then he paddled out into the foaming sea and back towards the village.

There was no sign of horrible Harald on the cliff top – only the stony scarecrow. Hilda had done her job well.

Eric netted a few more fish and arrived back at the village bridge at the same time as the warriors reached the great hall from the headland path and carried the two fallen warriors inside.

Eric pulled the coracle ashore. The fish-gutting could wait till later. The villagers from the huts and the fields were crowding into the great hall to see what was happening.

Rollo saw his thrall slip through but wasn't bothered. 'What's happening?' he asked Thorfinn as the two men entered the great hall.

'Seems they were practising a battle and Sigurd is hurt ... badly hurt,' Thorfinn told him.

'It will be that madman, Magnus, I bet,' Thorfinn's thin wife Freydis said.

The hall was packed. Someone was washing a wound on Magnus's head and the berserker was moaning softly.

But Sigurd lay on the platform. His leather jacket was cut away and his shirt pulled up to show a wound dripping blood. Women gathered round, shaking their heads, helpless. Freydis stepped forward and said, 'I know what to do. I've seen men with wounds like that from arrows.'

She stepped onto the platform and pointed at a grey-haired old woman. 'Hallbera, go and mix some warm porridge and stir in some raw onions.'

'Sounds awful,' the old woman said.

'Just do as I tell you!' Freydis ordered and the old woman shuffled off to obey her instructions.

'What are you doing, wife?' Thorfinn called. 'If you kill our leader they'll use you to practise their axe-throwing!' Others in the gloomy hall murmured their agreement.

Freydis looked at her husband and snarled her gap-toothed snarl. 'You have no more sense than one of the cows we carry from England, Thorfinn. You forget, I am from Iceland and the greatest of all the Norse sail from there. When I was a girl I sailed with Gunnbjörn Ulfsson.'

A gasp ran around the hall. Eric felt someone at his side and a voice said, 'What is she talking about?' It was Hilda.

'Gunnbjörn Ulfsson…' he whispered. 'My mother told me he was a great Norse sailor. He was caught in a storm between Norway and Greenland. He went so far west he found a new land! It was full of wild people who screamed as they attacked – the Norse call them Skraeling – screamers.'

'How is that?' you ask. 'If the Norse went west of Greenland they'd land in North America. Everyone knows Christopher Columbus discovered America!' Well, everyone is probably wrong. Old Chris C got there 600 years too late. He THOUGHT he discovered America – a bit like the boy who licked his nose with his tongue and THOUGHT he was the first person to do it. Maybe he was. But toads have been doing it for millions of years!

'What's she saying now?'

'She says the Skraeling attacked the Norse with arrows…' Eric listened to Freydis speaking. 'One warrior was struck in the stomach – just like Sigurd here. They carried him back to the ship and a wise old warrior said that if the arrow had entered his guts he would die. They should leave him and sail home. But if the arrow had not gone in too far he would live…'

'How could they tell?' Hilda asked.

'Wait … she's just coming to that bit … they fed the man porridge with onions…'

'That's what Hallbera has gone to make?'

'That's right,' Eric whispered. 'Here she is now.'

The crowd parted to let the old woman through. Freydis dipped a wooden spoon into the mess and held it to Sigurd's limp lips. She forced some of the mush of onion porridge in then held his mouth shut so he had to swallow.

'And now?' Thorfinn asked.

'And now ... we wait. If we place our noses to the wound we can sniff it. If we smell onion porridge then the wound has gone clean through. He will die.'

'No!' a deep voice groaned. Magnus staggered towards the platform. 'It wasn't my fault!'

'Well he wasn't stabbed by a starfish with a sea-shell, was he?' Freydis said, sharp as a wasp sting.

Magnus rubbed his aching head. 'I mean ... if the gods mean him to die he will die.'

'Yes, true,' the crowd breathed.

Sigurd opened his eyes and struggled to sit up. 'What is that smell?' he asked.

'Onion porridge,' Freydis said.

'But the smell is coming from my wound!'

'Oh!' the crowd sighed and looked at one another. 'Ohhhh, dear!'

Sigurd looked up to the heavy roof of reeds. Light spilled in through the hole that was cut to let the smoke go out. 'I can see the sky ... Valhalla,' he croaked. 'I am going to Valhalla.'

'You will fight with Thor at the battle of Ragnarok...' Magnus cried. 'You will beat trolls and giants and serpents and oh ... my head hurts!'

'My sword ... I need my sword,' Sigurd panted.

'We will bury you with your sword, my lord,' Rollo said. His voice was slimy as his fresh fish. 'We will give you everything a warrior needs in Valhalla ... a bow with arrows, food, armour.'

'A horse?'

'Ah ... no ... we ate the last one at harvest time.'

'Don't tell him that, you maggot! He is dying! Tell him we will bury him with a horse!' Freydis snapped.

'Sorry, sorry ... erm ... yes, we will get you a horse ... I mean, it may be a very small one ... in fact it may look a bit like a dead rat, but Thor won't mind!'

'And a servant,' Sigurd gurgled with his dying breath. 'A maiden to carry my weapons ... a beautiful woman to share my journey ... bury me with a maiden and ... and errrrkkkk!'

'What did he say?' Hilda asked.

'Bury me with a maiden and ... and errrrkkkk!' Eric said.

'What's errrrkkkk?'

'I don't know ... I think it was his dying breath.'

'Oh. Never mind. That's one less Viking to attack England,' Hilda grinned grimly.

Thorfinn had taken the stage next to his wife. 'Friends,' he said. 'The ships are almost ready to sail. We are waiting for a wind from the east.'

Everyone in the room nodded.

'While we are waiting we can bury Sigurd,' Thorfinn went on.

'Good idea,' Rollo put in. 'He'll start to smell if we leave it too long. Especially with that onion porridge pouring out of him. It's making me feel a bit sick.'

Thorfinn raised his voice so he would be heard. 'We

must send a maiden to Valhalla with him. The lucky, lucky woman will be his bride. She will marry Sigurd, serve him in the next life and live like a queen!'

'What's he saying?' Hilda asked.

'Shush! I'm listening,' Eric told her.

'Is there any man or woman here with a daughter – a fair maiden – who wants this great honour? Please don't fight over it – if you all want to send your daughters then we will have to draw lots to see who is lucky. Anyone?'

Little Harald had followed Hilda into the hall, wearing the cloak she had stitched for him. 'I have a big sister I can't stand!' he cried. 'You can have her!'

Rollo turned to the boy, shocked. 'No they can't!' he snapped.

'She's a nasty witch and I want to see her sacrificed like a sheep. In fact, if you give me the knife I'll do it for you!' he said.

'Harald be quiet! Your sister is promised to Askold the warrior. He would not be happy to see her have her throat cut then burned to ashes!'

Harald stuck out his tongue and blew. 'Pttthhhht!'

One by one men and women stepped forward to explain just why their daughter was not free to die by knife and flame.

'What are they saying?' Hilda hissed.

'I'll tell you later,' Eric promised. 'Wait…'

Freydis stepped over the corpse of Sigurd as he lay there on the platform. 'It is a huge honour to give a girl as a sacrifice. The family that gives the girl will be blessed with good luck … and the warrior Vikings will be blessed with good winds.'

'So you give a daughter to be burned on the funeral fire with Sigurd?' Rollo asked.

Freydis's face split into her broken-toothed grin. 'I have no daughter...'

'Then you shouldn't be telling the rest of us what to do!' the fisherman snorted.

'I have no daughter ... but I do have a thrall-maiden. She is not exactly beautiful ... but she will do.'

'You'd give her up?' someone asked. 'Something that precious?'

Freydis shrugged, 'As the Norse proverb says, it is easier to look after a hundred sheep than one girl. I'll be glad to be rid of her!'

The eyes of every villager and warrior in the room turned towards Hilda.

Hilda looked hard at Eric. 'Now will you tell me what they are saying?' she demanded.

'Ah – er ... you don't want to know, Hilda. You really don't want to know!'

There is an Old Norse saying, 'He who wishes to leap high must take a long run.' Hilda should have learned it. Because if Hilda didn't take a long run ... very soon ... then she was in for the high jump and no mistake. On the other hand, Eric was saved from the sea at the end of Chapter 1. Maybe Hilda will be saved from the sword at the end of this chapter. Who knows? I certainly don't.

Marriage, Mead and Misery

Why is everyone looking at me and smiling?' Hilda asked.

'They are happy for you,' Eric said carefully.

'That's nice. Why?'

'Because you are going to get married!'

'Am I? I didn't notice anyone asking to marry me. I must have been asleep at the time,' Hilda sneered. 'Well?'

'Well what?'

'Well,' she said and jabbed a finger into Eric's shoulder with every word she said. 'Who – am – I – going – to – marry?'

Eric cleared his throat. 'Sigurd.'

Hilda looked up at the ceiling. 'Maybe you haven't noticed,' she said. 'But they are too late. Sigurd is dead. He is dead as a duck's toenail. He has turned up his toes and is half way to Hell by now ... or wherever dead Vikings go.'

'Valhalla,' Eric said.

'Whatever,' the girl said. 'I cannot marry a dead man. Can I?'

'Yes.'

'What?'

'If the Vikings say you can, then you can.'

'What a jolly marriage that will be!' Hilda laughed. 'What shall we talk about today, dear husband? The weather? Yes, it's dead cold, but I like the cold because your rotting body doesn't smell so bad. Hah!'

'Calm down, Hilda, or they will get upset. Just smile and do everything they tell you. I'll think of a way out of it.'

The girl looked at him sharply. 'Out of what? Is there something else you haven't told me?'

Eric turned to Hilda. 'No ... nothing at all!'

The men in the hall started to lift Sigurd's body and strip off his clothes. Women hurried in with cloths and water to wash the blood off his corpse. The village weaver brought some fine blue cloth to make his funeral robes. Freydis seemed to take charge and started cutting the cloth with shears and giving women the task of sewing the pieces into a suit.

The old woman, Hallbera, had been out of the great hall and came back with a dress of fine green linen. She held it in front of Hilda.

'Nice,' the girl nodded. Hallbera bowed and started measuring Hilda the way Freydis had been measuring the dead warrior chief.

'Your wedding gown,' Eric told her.

Hilda sighed. 'I suppose, as queen, I will have lots of wealth. All Sigurd's gold and his thralls?'

'Oh ... yes,' Eric told her. 'You'll be the richest girl in Norway!' he laughed a hollow laugh. 'Until they burn you to ashes, of course,' he said to himself.

Freydis was pleased with her new position of power. She had given her thrall-girl as the corpse's queen so now she had the right to order people around. 'There are some people here just standing around and doing nothing,' she said with a fierce glare.

Magnus rose slowly to his feet. 'I've got a bad head. It hurts!' he said.

'And it serves you right,' Freydis snapped back. 'It was you that got us into this mess. What were you thinking of? Stabbing your own chief?'

'I wasn't thinking,' the monstrous man said miserably. 'I was in a berserker trance. I don't remember a thing! Sorry.'

'What's done is done. You know what the Norse wise women say?'

'No.'

'It is no use mending a fence after the child has fallen down the well,' Freydis told him.

'You want me to repair the fence round the well?' Magnus asked.

'No, I don't,' Freydis sighed. 'I have another job for you. You will need a dozen warriors to help you. Come over here!' she ordered.

Magnus rambled across to her and she began speaking quickly in a voice too low for Eric to hear. Magnus nodded, gathered warriors around him and left the hall.

Dead Sigurd was being dressed and placed on the throne at the end of the hall. An empty throne stood next to him.

As the women stitched Hilda into the new gown and decorated it with bear teeth and glass beads Eric spoke to her quickly in English. 'Listen to me but don't look surprised.'

'Very well, thrall-boy,' she replied with a smile.

'The death of Sigurd will make no difference. The people are starving. The attack on an English monastery will go ahead in the next few days. If we are going to escape it has to be soon. Tonight.'

'Yes … but I am going to be a rich queen,' Hilda said.

Eric tried to keep his face calm. 'Listen, you evil, greedy witch-child … the Vikings will show no mercy. If it's Tyneside they attack then it's your mother they'll kill or make a thrall. It's her blood that will be on your hands … no! No! Keep smiling! No one else can save England.'

'You can.'

'I need your help. I don't WANT your help – I would rather sail with Sigurd to Valhalla than have your help. But I need you … that's the only reason I'm going to rescue you!'

Hilda smiled and brushed threads off her dress. 'Rescue me from the life of a queen?'

Eric bit his lip. To tell her about the plan to burn her would make her panic. He needed her to stay calm and cheerful … a bride going gladly to her wedding.

'This noon-tide you marry Sigurd. This afternoon they have a feast – as much as the starving people can spare –

then tomorrow, at dawn, they burn Sigurd,' the boy said.

'And your plan is?'

'My plan is to sail back to England … no! Keep smiling!'

'In your coracle?!' Hilda asked … smiling. 'Then you can go alone. Have you seen the waves out there? I'd rather stay warm in the village.'

'Oh, they'll keep you warm alright,' Eric said savagely. He took a deep breath. 'You marry Sigurd…'

'So you said.'

'Then you have the feast this afternoon.'

'I know.'

'But all that eating and drinking makes people want to use the toilet pit,' Eric went on, blushing a little.

'So?'

'So … when it grows dark you tell the crowd that you are going to the pit. By then they will all be drunk except you and me. That's when we escape.'

'But they will miss me if I don't come back,' Hilda argued and lifted her foot to let Hallbera slip on a green slipper to match the dress.

'Remember how you got Harald to trick me?'

'We made a dummy Harald out of rocks,' Hilda nodded.

'So we make a dummy Hilda out of sticks and straw. We slip it onto the throne and it will be morning before they find you've gone. We will have a night's start on them.'

Hilda shook her head. 'But the stone dummy DIDN'T fool you,' she argued.

'Because I was not drunk.'

Hilda blew out her cheeks. 'So we escape. But how do we get back to England?'

'In a ship,' Eric said simply.

'Do you have one?'

'I'll steal one.'

'From where?'

'From South Bay.'

'A Viking ship? Can you sail one?' Hilda gasped then remembered to keep smiling.

'I can sail anything,' Eric said. 'Ships are in our blood on Wearside.'

'That must make their sails red and sticky,' Hilda said.

Eric went on, 'But South Bay is sheltered. I need to row the longship out into the sea to catch the wind. Then I can raise the sail. I need someone on another oar to help me. Once we are at sea you can leave the rest to me.'

'It'll never work,' Hilda said.

'It has to,' Eric said. 'It's a matter of life and death!'

What he didn't say was whose death...

***

The afternoon was spent in bustle and bother as the villagers ran in and out of the great hall. They brought planks for tables and each brought the food they could spare. For some it was not much.

Hallbera showed her gums in a toothless grin to Hilda. 'This is my last bag of corn,' she said. She spoke slowly so Hilda could understand enough words and make sense of the Norse tongue. In her long life she'd learned a few English words too. 'But our Vikings will soon be back with enough food to fatten us all through the winter.'

'If their plan works,' Hilda said sourly.

'Oh, but it will!' Hallbera cackled. 'The gods will be so pleased with the sacrifice they'll send strong winds.'

'Sacrifice?' Hilda asked, struggling with the word. 'A killing?'

'Hee! Hee! Didn't they tell you?' Hallbera giggled. 'Didn't they tell you?'

'Tell me?'

'You are the sacrifice!'

Hilda frowned. She must have heard it wrong. 'I am giving the sacrifice? Oh, they're taking one of my six sheep?' She sighed. 'Oh, well, once I'm queen I'll have a hundred sheep,' she said in English. Then, in her rough Norse, she tried to tell Hallbera, 'I am happy to give sacrifice.'

The old woman shook her head in wonder, 'Brave girl!'

'Eh?'

But Hilda and Hallbera had to move as fresh rushes were spread on the floor. They covered up the stale ale that had been spilled, the dog droppings that had been left behind ... and worse.

Worse? What can be worse than eating in a room with dog droppings on the floor? I hope you are not eating a meal as I tell you this. If you are then stop and take a deep breath. It wasn't just the dogs that left droppings in a Viking hall. Some of the humans got very drunk and couldn't be bothered to take a trip to the toilet pit. Know what I mean? Right. Get back to your tasty tea-time treats!

Freydis shouted orders. And the noise rose to the roof as people hurried around, preparing the feast. Rollo sent Eric off to fetch the fresh fish and gut them and lay them at the edge of the fire to cook.

Only one person sat quietly in a corner. It was a large corner because he was a large man. He rubbed at the sore spot on his head.

A warrior carried a horn full of honey beer – or 'mead' as the English monks called it – and sat beside him. 'Well, Magnus are you going to start drinking?'

The berserker shook his head. 'No. My head aches, Helgi the Sly.'

The warrior called Helgi seemed to be the new leader since Sigurd had died. But he wasn't as handsome as Sigurd – in fact his little eyes were too close together and his mouth was mean and thin. He looked the sort of man who would cut your finger off to steal your ring. 'A drink will cheer you up,' Helgi told Magnus. 'Maybe later you will go berserk and start a fight! That will be fun!'

'No. I don't think so,' Magnus rumbled.

'You love a good fight,' the warrior Helgi reminded him.

'I hate fighting. I got angry. I fought and I killed. Once I took off the heads of three men with one swing of my axe.'

'That's why you are our hero, Magnus,' the other man laughed.

'But ... what if I can't get angry?' the berserker asked.

'Can't?'

'That ... that blow to my head!'

'Ah! That was Gardar Svavarsson from Sweden! You can have real fun smashing him with your sword!'

'No ... I mean ... I don't feel angry any more. The hit on the head ... like taking a stick to an angry dog ... it calmed me down!'

Helgi the Sly emptied the horn of mead down his throat and laughed. 'A berserker without his anger? Hah! What use is that? Eh? Magnus? What use is that?'

As the man walked away, Magnus muttered, 'No use at all. A berserker without anger and a Viking who kills his own leader! I'll never get to Valhalla.' He gave a sigh that shook the walls, and mice in the wattle walls squeaked in fear.

But Magnus was the only gloom in the room. Everyone else was growing more and more excited.

Sorry. You are quite right. Not EVERYONE was getting excited. Sigurd wasn't getting excited. He looked wonderful in his wedding robes, of course. But he didn't look excited. All I can say is that he WOULD have been excited if he was alive. But he wasn't ... so he wasn't.

DWARFS, A DUMMY AND DARKNESS

The whole village and the warriors were crowded into the great hall.

> When I say the WHOLE village I don't mean the thralls - like Cinderella they didn't get invited to posh people's parties. Thralls were just 'objects' to the Norse ... like a table or a toilet bowl is to you. And you wouldn't take a toilet bowl to a party, would you? Eh? You WOULD?! They say there are some strange people in the world. I guess you are one of them ... and you won't be invited to my next party.

A fire had been lit to keep out the chill of the winter evening and the smoke drifted up to the roof. A little smoke seeped through the hole at the top but most of it fell back and filled the hall with a faint fog.

That pleased Eric. The fog and the strong mead would muddle the minds of the Norse people. No one would notice the switch. And if all the warriors were in the hall then no one was guarding the ten dragon ships on the shore of South Bay.

A bent-backed old man climbed onto the platform and rattled a walking stick for silence. 'Friends!' he cried. 'As I am the wise man of this village I have been asked to take on the duty of marrying the happy couple and of seeing to the sacrifice.'

'What's he saying?' Hilda asked Eric as they stood at the side of the platform. 'He used that word like "killing" again … the same as Hallbera did.'

'Oh … nothing much. He's talking about how a married couple are joined till death,' Eric lied.

'Pah!' the girl spat. 'Then it's already the shortest marriage in the world.'

The old man was saying, 'Can I ask the lucky, happy, bride to step up and take her place on the platform?' The man looked around with watery eyes.

'That's you,' Eric said, nudging the English girl.

'What do I do?'

'Oh … sit on the throne next to Sigurd,' Eric said.

Hilda climbed onto the platform and in the light of twenty flickering lanterns, through the smoky air, she almost looked beautiful. And she felt beautiful too. She walked to the throne delicately, like a doe deer and sat down. 'Pleased to meet you, Sigurd,' she said politely.

Sigurd didn't reply ... which is not so polite.

'Take your master's hand in yours,' the wise man told her.

'What?'

The man lifted Hilda's hand and placed it on the cold and lifeless hand of Sigurd. 'Urrrgh!' she shivered. 'I hope your riches are so great it is worth all this horror,' she told her bridegroom.

The lantern-light glinted in his eyes but his lips didn't move.

'Helga. Do you take this man to be your husband?' the man asked.

'Eh?'

Eric spoke loudly. 'He said, "Helga. Do you take this man to be your husband?"'

'My name isn't Helga!'

'Oh, just say jah!' Eric said. 'Get it over with. The sooner you finish the quicker we get away and the more time we have.'

'Jah!' Hilda said.

'My Lord Sigurd. Do you take this woman to be your wife?' he asked.

'Jah!' came the reply.

Hilda screamed and dropped the dead man's hand.

'Calm down!' Eric urged. 'There is someone standing behind Sigurd's throne to give the answers. Nothing to worry about!'

'Worry? I almost wet myself!' Hilda said and her cheeks burned with anger.

'Save it till you need to go to the toilet pit,' Eric joked.

Hilda gave him a glare that could kill a cat at twenty paces.

The wise man was rambling about the happy life the couple would have together in Valhalla.

'What is that?' Hilda asked.

'He's talking about Valhalla … it's the hall of the dead,' Eric explained. 'Now be quiet.'

The whole hall was silent as the old man told the tale the warriors knew so well.

'Tomorrow at sunrise the happy young pair will sail off until they reach the gates of Valhalla. And the poet-gods shall greet them and show them in to the hall with 540 doors!'

The crowd gasped in wonder.

'The valkyries will fly like ravens and choose the bravest of the brave – those who died in battle!' the old man cried.

Picture it. Valkyries flew over the battlefield and gathered the bravest of the dead warriors. They ALSO served drink at the tables of the gods. Picking up dead bodies? Then serving drinks? I hope they washed their hands before they served the drinks.

'Sigurd didn't exactly die in battle did he?' little Harald said to his father as they stood by the fire.

'Hush, Harald!' Rollo said.

'Valhalla will hold the bravest 800. Every day the 800 will ride out to battle with the giants on the plains of

Asgard. Those who die bravely will return to Valhalla and be brought back to life. They will feed on roast boar and drink the finest ales. That is what is waiting for lucky Sigurd ... and his bride will, of course be there to welcome him home from battle!'

The villagers clapped. Hilda smiled ... though she didn't know why.

Suddenly the old man's voice rose to a crackling screech. 'Those who do NOT die bravely will go to Hell...'

Gasp!

'... and those who drown at sea will, of course go to Aegir's Hall at the bottom of the sea.'

Ahhhh!

In his quiet corner the berserker frowned. 'Aegir's Hall ... that's where a berserker belongs when he can't go berserk any longer. But how do I get there?' He sighed and turned his fat face to the platform.

The wise man was looking brightly at Hilda. 'We can't have one of you going to Aegir's Hall while the other goes to Valhalla, can we? That means we have to make quite sure the young lady is quite dead before we send her out to the sea at sunrise!' He gave a small laugh. The villagers laughed. Hilda laughed ... though she didn't know why.

'And now, my friends, no wedding is a wedding without the wedding singer!'

Ooooh!

'Tonight we are lucky enough to have a poet all the way from Kaupang. Let's have a big round of applause for the great ... the one and only ... the poet's poet ... Björn Ironside!'

The crowd cheered and whistled and a heavy man with a beard as thick as a thorn-bush climbed onto the platform. He bowed to the married couple. Hilda bowed back. Sigurd didn't.

'Tonight, my friends, I would like to tell you the terrible tale of the Giant Gilling!'

Hooray!

Drinking horns were filled. Fish was scooped from the ashes round the fire and chomped. Villagers settled down to hear the tale of Giant Gilling. Hilda was sitting behind the storyteller Björn Ironside, who was standing at the front of the stage. She couldn't move. If she did the whole of the hall would see her and wonder where she was going. She gave a little hand shrug to Eric and he waved for her to wait.

Björn Ironside had a large voice to go with his large face. His yellow teeth glinted in the lantern-light as he smiled at the captive crowd.

'Here we are in Midgard, it's the place that we call home. Of all the evil creatures that ever lived the worst were two cruel dwarfs ... everybody knows the names of the dwarfs were...'

The crowd cried out, 'Fjalar and Galar!'

'Fjalar and Galar,' Björn Ironside nodded. 'Now, one day Giant Gilling came to call on these two deadly dwarfs. This Gilling was a gentle giant, as giants go, and tried to never hurt a beetle. But Giant Gilling was a giant and giants eat an awful lot!'

Ahhhh, they do, the crowd agreed ... although they'd never met one.

'To make things worse the giant took along his wife. They ate and ate and ate some more.'

The poet made himself look small and ugly ... the last was easy. He put on squeaky voices and played the parts of both the dwarfs. '"That Gilling eats a fearful lot!" said Fjalar. "An awful lot!" his brother agreed. "If he and his big wife go on like this we won't have any food left," Galar grumbled. "I think we should get rid of him!" And so they made their deadly plot!

'First they said they had a present for their guest. They gave the giant a huge millstone on a rope. A necklace, they said, to hang around his neck. Oh, how the giant loved the big stone circle hanging and banging against his mighty chest. And then the dwarfs said they would like to sail out to sea to get a breath of good sea air...'

Hahhhh! The quiet crowd breathed – they knew just what was coming next!

Do you? I mean to say, we all have people call to visit that seem to stay too long. No matter what you do they never take a hint and go. Even if you lie back in your chair and fall asleep. But you are not an evil dwarf ... at least you don't look like a dwarf, though you could be evil. The point is YOU wouldn't do what they did next in this old Viking story. I hope. Not if it's me visiting, anyway!

'No sooner had this putrid pair sailed out into the deepest open sea than they pointed down into the depths and cried, "Look there, old Gilling. Look down there! The Hall of Aegir right below!" The giant looked down from the boat and stretched his neck and as he stretched the two dwarfs pushed him. Gilling fell and Gilling splashed and Gilling tried his best to swim. But no one swims that well when there's a millstone round their neck. The bubbles rose as Gilling sank and that's the last they saw of him!'

Björn took a deep drink of mead and carried on. 'They went back to their seaside cave and hoped that Mrs Gilling would go home. They told her that her dear husband was dead. But, sad to say, she didn't move, she simply sat right down and cried. And giant tears sloshed down and round and filled up half the cruel dwarfs' cave! That's when they came up with another plan. Fjalar stood up on the cliffs above the door into the cave. He held another mighty millstone. "I want to show you where your loving husband drowned," the wicked Galar told Mrs Gilling. As soon as she stepped out of the door, Fjalar dropped the great millstone – it landed on the woman's head – her skull was crushed. She dropped down dead!'

Oooof! The crowd cried, loving every horrid moment.

***

Mad Magnus (who wasn't as mad as he used to be) rose quietly and slipped out of the door. He walked through the dark, damp paths of the village to the miller's house. Every day the miller struggled to turn the massive millstone that ground the corn to make the flour. But Magnus picked it up as you might pick up a pebble on the beach.

Then he walked to the house of Rollo the fisherman and found a length of ship's rope by the door. 'Good,' he grunted and headed off into the night.

***

Hilda shuffled on her throne. It was time to make the switch and get away. But still the poet prattled about the dwarfs and the giants. It seemed the Giant Gilling had a son called Sattung, and Sattung went looking for his dead mum and dad. When he found they were dead he plotted a terrible revenge.

'Giant Sattung picked up Fjalar and Galar by their dirty necks and carried them out to sea. He carried them far out till the water rose up to his own shoulders. And then he placed the wicked dwarfs upon a bare and grassless rock. He told the dwarfs that when the tide came in they'd have to swim back home. "It's much too far!" they cried. "Well then, you'll have to drown," the giant laughed.'

The poet, Björn Ironside, looked around the lantern-lit crowd and smiled. Then he looked at Hilda and Sigurd on their thrones. 'And so, it's as the ancient proverb says … do not put up with evil, but fight it and do good!'

Then he turned back to the crowd. 'Now fill your cups and drink to the health of our great lord and his new bride!'

The villagers and the warriors crowded round the barrels of ale and mead that stood near the fire. And Hilda took the chance to slip silently into the shadows. Eric was waiting by the back door to the hall.

Hilda tore off the green dress and slipped into some old trousers, a shirt and a cloak while Eric pulled the dress onto the dummy of sticks and straw.

'I found some dye in the weaver's house,' Eric told her. 'I painted a face on the dummy!'

Light spilled out from the open door and lit the gruesome face on a cloth head. 'It's so ugly,' Hilda shuddered.

'Yes!' Eric cried. 'I wanted it to look like you!'

Hilda looked around for a stick to thrash the young monk with but he slipped into the hall to put the dummy on the throne. The dress had a hood. He pulled it over the ugly head and placed the five-fingered hand of sticks into Sigurd's five-fingered hand of dead flesh. The villagers were happily drinking and eating around the fire and the foggy fug of fire-smoke was thicker than ever. No one noticed Eric make the switch. Everything was going to plan.

He went back to the door where Hilda was waiting. A soft sound made her go stiff as her husband's hand. 'Someone is coming this way,' she whispered to the boy.

Everything had stopped going to plan…

A BERSERKER, A BAY AND A BOAT OF LIFE

They pressed themselves into the shadows of the wall and watched as a giant figure passed through the light of the doorway.

'Magnus the Berserker,' Eric breathed.

'What was he carrying?'

'Some sort of stone – a circle with a hole in the middle.'

'A millstone?'

'Yes.'

'Where is he going?'

'He's taking the path leading south,' Eric said straining his eyes into the dull air.

'But we want to go that way to South Bay,' Hilda moaned.

'No. We'll go to the stream and take the coracle. I want to take it with us and there's no point carrying it over the headland.'

'I'm not going on the water in that shabby little, tatty little, pathetic little, miserable little so-called boat!'

'Fine,' Eric said. 'So swim.'

You can insult a man's socks. Tell him they smell like a cowpat from Hell. You can insult his taste in ties or his taste in pies. But you cannot insult his car, his boat or his toy plane ... or any of his vehicles. Men love vehicles more than they love train-spotting. Insult his coracle and he may never forgive you. Oh, Hilda, how could you?!

He turned on his heel and marched down to the bridge. Hilda ran after him, grumbling and stumbling.

If they had stayed a few moments longer they may have seen that the large shadow of the berserker had its own smaller shadow.

The wind whipped the stream till it bubbled like a pot of porridge.

'It's cold,' Hilda said shivering inside her cloak.

'It's wonderful,' Eric said. 'The Vikings were going to make a sacrifice to the gods to ask for a friendly wind.'

'Friendly!' Hilda laughed harshly.

'Yes, can't you feel it? The wind has swung round to the east. It is blowing straight to England! Once we're at sea we'll race over the ocean. We could be home in a day. Our God wants us to escape ... and he doesn't need a sacrifice.'

'What sacrifice?' Hilda asked.

'Oh ... nothing,' Eric said and picked up the coracle and placed it at the edge of the stream. 'Climb in.'

Hilda stepped carefully into the little boat and it rocked on the ripples of the stream. Eric pulled the paddle free and climbed in after her. He let the stream carry them out to sea then turned south. He kept as close to the shore as he could and it was fairly calm in the shelter of the land.

The headland loomed high above them and currents made the waters crash and chop against the coracle. Hilda closed her eyes and held on to the sides. If she had opened her eyes and looked up she would have seen the fat figure of the berserker walking the last half a league to the cliff top above them.

But it was dark and he was no more than a shadow on the sleet-filled clouds. And the shadow still had its own shadow.

Eric turned the coracle into South Bay and found it was sheltered and quite calm. The mountains behind kept the east winds away from the dark waters. 'A good place to build a fleet,' he said. 'Well hidden. Even if an English trader sailed past he wouldn't see the dragon ships. England would be in for a shock like a bolt of lightning ... if it wasn't for us!'

Hilda told him sourly, 'We aren't there yet … and we still don't know which monastery they plan to attack … and we still don't know if the English can raise an army to stop them.'

Eric paddled and sighed. 'You could try to be a bit more cheerful, Hilda.'

'I'll be cheerful when I see my mother safe from those Viking swords. Now hurry up.'

The tide was flowing out. It would make sailing a longship out of the bay much easier but Eric struggled to push the little leather boat against the tide. At last he reached the beach.

'This is the ship they used to make the practice attack,' Eric said as he helped the girl onto the shore. It was the one closest to the water.

'And how do we get it back into the water?' she snapped. 'It's huge.'

'I know,' Eric said, 'but that wind is blowing out to sea. I thought if we raised the sail, the wind would drag us over the beach and into deeper water.'

'You thought that, did you?' Hilda said and it annoyed him almost as much as the insult to his coracle.

'It may not work … but we have to try it.'

'To save England?'

'And to save your miserable…'

'What?'

'Nothing,' he snapped. 'Take one of the oars and push when I tell you to.'

Hilda picked up an oar and stumbled to the stern of the ship. 'What are these boxes on the floor?'

'I suppose that's where they sit when they row,' Eric shrugged as he sorted the ropes at the foot of the mast. He'd never seen this type of ship before but he knew that it would work in the same way as the fishing and trading ships back on the River Wear.

While Hilda waited she crouched down to look at one of the boxes. It had a leather hinge on one side. It meant the top lifted up. She opened it. 'Oh, Eric, look at this!' she cried.

'I'm busy.'

'No! This is perfect! So perfect! I really think we are meant to escape.'

Have you noticed this is the second time someone has said they are sure to escape? This can only mean one of three things. One, they are meant to escape. Or, two, you should never open your big mouth too soon. Or, three, it doesn't mean anything at all. Who knows?

Eric hauled on a rope and the sail began to slide up the mast. He sighed. 'What is it?'

'These boxes that they sit on. They are chests. They have weapons in and food. Lots of food! Look ... dried fish, cheeses, bread ... I'm starving! I had to watch all those people in the village have a feast while I sat on the throne.'

At least she meant to say that but with fish and cheese crammed into her mouth, what she really said was,

'Mmmmf! Mm-mm-mmmff-mmff-um-mum!'

Eric let the sail rise gently and it caught the wind. The whole of the boat shuddered and the dragon nose seemed to rise to sniff the air. The mast strained and bent forward. The ship shifted on the round, sea-washed pebbles and jerked forward. It moved again and started to get enough speed to move smoothly after the ebbing tide.

The dragon's breast ploughed into the water and the whole ship leapt on the next wave.

'We're afloat!' Eric cried. He ran to the stern of the boat and fell over Hilda but snatched at the coracle and hauled it on board as they raced past it on the beach.

'You don't need that bundle of twigs now you have a real ship!' Hilda laughed.

Eric scowled but said nothing. He picked his way through the Viking chests to the sail ropes and tugged one to bring the ship away from the headland. Then he went to the back of the ship and tied the steering paddle to lock it in place. He couldn't trust Hilda to steer till they were out of the bay and it was daylight. Then he'd teach her how to do it. Meanwhile he had to try and sail a ship alone – a ship meant for two dozen men of muscle.

'Ohh!' he sighed as they slid through the gentle waves towards the open sea. 'It's beautiful. When I get home I'm going to build ships like this! It's the most beautiful thing I've ever sailed.'

Hilda was still eating. 'Mmmmf! Mm-mm-mmmff-mmff-um-mum!' she said. They were just under the headland and fifty paces from the sea.

Forty paces. Thirty. Twenty. A snail could crawl those

last few lengths. But not in a sinking ship it couldn't…

***

Mad Magnus rested the millstone on the turf at the top of the headland. He muttered the wise words of the warrior to himself. 'A berserker without his anger? Hah! What use is that? Eh? Magnus? What use is that?'

Magnus took the rope and threaded it through the hole in the middle of the millstone. Then he made a loop around his neck. 'Even Giant Gilling couldn't swim with a millstone round his neck,' Magnus said to the sea.

He picked up the stone in his powerful arms and slowly raised it above his head. He stepped forward to the edge of the cliff. 'I am going to the Hall of Aegir at the bottom of the sea! I do not deserve Valhalla and the heroes. I'm just a bad berserker. Hall of Aegir, here I come!' he cried.

It was dark, of course. Magnus could not see the sea, you see? He could not see the tide was rushing out. Below him was a pebble beach. Anyone who threw themselves off would not go 'Splash' to the Hall of Aegir. No, they would go 'Crunch' and end up with a pile of pebbles up their nose. Magnus was not just a bad berserker. He wasn't even good at killing himself.

Magnus threw the millstone.
The millstone soared into the night wind till it reached the end of the rope.

The millstone ripped at the rope. It was Rollo's rope and Rollo was a very mean man. He never bought new rope till the old rope was worn out. And it was the worn-out rope that Magnus had found by the fisherman's back door.

Of course it snapped.

Magnus stood at the top of the headland and wondered why he wasn't in the Hall of Aegir.

The millstone soared through the air towards the beach. It struck a large rock and bounced like ... like a millstone off a rock.

It leapt back out over the sea and landed in the sea. But first it hit a dragon's head on the front of a longship.

Eric and Hilda heard the crash and in the dim light saw the dragon's head shatter and vanish into the sea.

The bows of the ship were torn and open. The next wave gushed in and slowed the speeding longship to a stop. Water rushed along towards the two young sailors. They could see the safety of the shore but it was thirty paces of deep iced water away. Even a good swimmer could drown.

'I can't swim!' Hilda cried.

Eric spread his hands, 'And I'm not strong enough to swim in that cold water and fight the currents.'

'I'll drown!' the girl wailed.

'Ahhh!' Eric sighed. 'I won't!'

'You won't?'

'No, I have my coracle,' he said as he turned it the right way up and sat in it. He waited as the ship began to sink below him and the coracle floated on the rising water.

'Wait for me!' Hilda called as she hastily waded through the water towards him.

'Oh, no,' he shouted. 'You don't want to sail in a shabby little, tatty little, pathetic little, miserable little so-called boat!'

'It's a lovely boat,' she said grasping the side as the freezing sea slapped at her knees.

'A bundle of twigs.'

'A beautiful work of art,' she said and dragged a numb leg into the coracle. Eric pulled her aboard just as the longship lurched deeper towards its death.

'Even the finest ship should have a special coracle aboard to save shipwrecked sailors,' he said as he paddled towards the safety of the shore.

'Yes,' Hilda agreed. 'It would save lives. We could call it a "boat of life".'

'Life-boat sounds better,' Eric argued.

'Hah!' Hilda scoffed. 'No one would EVER call a pathetic bundle of twigs like this a life-boat!'

They were still arguing when they reached the village bridge and pulled the coracle ashore.

SMOKE, SIGURD AND
A SECRET

ric and Hilda were still arguing as he pulled the
lifeboat up into the shelter of the bridge and they
ran up the slope to the great hall.

'Boat of life!'

'Life-boat!'

'Boat of life!'

'Life-boat!'

It was a titanic argument.

'What now?' Hilda asked.

'I'll think of something,' Eric snapped.

'But what?'

'Something.'

In the smoky hall Eric stole the dummy from the stage.
'Where are you taking the queen?' old Hallbera asked.

'To the toilet pit,' Eric lied.

'Can't she go by herself?'

'Too drunk,' the young monk told her.

'Disgraceful. I don't approve of dildren chinking!'
Hallbera said as she slobbered ale down her wrinkled
chin.

'Dildren chinking?' Eric frowned.

'Yesh ... dildren like Hilda duddent shrink!'

'You're drunk,' Eric snapped.

'Yush ... but at least I don't need shum-buddy to take
me for a widdle!' the woman snapped back. At least, as

snappy as you can be when you haven't any teeth.

Outside Hilda took off the soaking trousers and slipped back into the fine wedding dress. She climbed onto the platform and headed back to the throne.

Hallbera called, 'Did you enjoy that?'

'No,' Hilda barked back. 'I got my feet wet.'

'Ahhhh!' the old woman nodded. 'I do that all the time these days. They don't make toilet pits like they used to when I was a girl!'

'Eh?'

'Duddent shrink!' Hallbera said and fell off the platform onto the rushes on the floor. She lay there and snored. That was very handy because Thorfinn was able to use her as a step to climb up onto the platform.

'Friends, warriors, countrymen ... can I have your attention please? I have something very important to say!'

Ooooh!

'I have been talking with the warriors. The last ships will be finished by sunset tomorrow. They can all sail tomorrow night on the evening tide!'

Hooray!

'This means the boat-builders are free to build a new boat – a new knorr for me and Freydis.'

'What's wrong with the old one?' someone called.

'It's as leaky as a drinking horn made from knitted wool,' a woman laughed.

Thorfinn raised his chin and said proudly, 'It is a fine ship that has sailed the North Sea many times. It was this ship,' he went on showing a little anger, 'that found the monastery our Vikings will attack tomorrow. If ships were warriors then my ship would be a hero!'

The crowd in the smoky hall had gone quiet now and some began to mutter that Thorfinn made sense.

'So my ship should die like a hero – it should die like Sigurd and his bride!'

'How?' someone called.

'In a land to the east called Rus they send their Viking heroes to Valhalla in a ship.'

'No, no!' A warrior cut in. 'If he sinks he'll end up in the Hall of Aegir at the bottom of the sea. He has to burn and rise with the smoke to Valhalla!'

Thorfinn grinned. 'I know!' he said. 'We send the ship out on the morning tide and set fire to it.'

'Ahhhh!'

'Sigurd and the hero ship go to Valhalla together!' Freydis shouted. 'My husband is the cleverest man in the village!'

'What about the bride?' Hallbera asked. She sat up from the rushes where she'd been sleeping and pointed to Hilda on the throne.

'I've thought of that too,' Thorfinn said. 'She sails with her husband. This village has an Angel of Death – an elder woman who will strangle the bride first.'

'That's me!' Hallbera said happily. 'I am the Angel of Death for this village.'

Freydis bowed to her and went on, 'The girl's body goes out to be swallowed in the flames. The lucky, lucky thrall dies a glorious, happy death!'

'My husband is the cleverest man in Norway!' Freydis laughed.

The villagers began to clap and cheer Thorfinn.

Hilda had seen Hallbera point at her and seen the crowd turn, smiling, towards her. She gave Eric a signal to come towards her. 'What is Thorfinn saying?'

'Err … he is saying … he is saying that … erm … Sigurd is to be buried at sea, not on a fire. He will be pushed out on the morning tide in Thorfinn's trading ship.'

'And me?'

'Ah … you will go with him.'

'Why?'

'Oh … ah … to throw him over the side,' Eric said thinking quickly.

'Then I'll be adrift in the North Sea,' Hilda cried.

'Yes … but I have a plan.'

'A plan to save me?'

'A plan to save you … and save England at the same time!'

Hilda sat back on the throne, content. 'I am pleased. I saved your miserable life so now you can save mine. You owe me, thrall-monk.

> How unfair is that? This wretched girl MAY have saved Eric from the sea. But she was well paid when she swapped him for six sheep. Eric owes her nothing. In fact, it would serve her right if he left her to burn in the knorr. He could save himself ... and just ig-knorr her!

So, what is the plan?'

Before he could answer, a small voice cried out near the door, 'Make way! Make way! I have terrible news!'

The crowd parted and let the little figure of Harald step through the smoky air and take his place on the stage.

'What's happened, son?' Rollo asked.

'One of the Viking fleet of ships has been sunk!'

The villagers gave a great groan.

'I followed Mad Magnus to the top of the headland at South Bay. One of the longships drifted past and I saw him throw a millstone down and sink it!'

Everyone was shocked and suddenly sober.

'It's true,' came the rumbling voice of Magnus from the door.

Rollo jumped onto the platform next to his son. 'Magnus could have wrecked our plans. Now we have to sail with nine ships. What shall we do with him?'

'Banish him,' the warrior Helgi the Sly said. 'He's a

berserker who doesn't go berserk and he killed Sigurd. Now he's sunk a ship. He's worse than useless.'

Hallbera staggered to her feet. 'He has fought and saved you many times. To me he is a hero!' she croaked.

'Thanks, Mum,' Magnus muttered.

'So here's what I say ... send him out with Sigurd and the thrall-girl to burn on the ship. In fact Magnus can strangle the girl before he sets them all on fire, can't you, son?'

'Yes, Mum.'

Hallbera nodded happily. 'Then Sigurd will arrive at Valhalla with a bride and a warrior to fight with him. Of course I will miss my son, Magnus...'

'Thanks Mum,'

'But at least I won't have to keep trying to fill that fat face of his,' she muttered.

The villagers seemed to like that idea. And so it was decided.

The barrels of mead and ale were empty and the flickering fire as dead as Sigurd. The feast was finished and some people had begun to drift home. Others just curled up on the rushes and fell asleep in the smoky warmth of the great hall.

Dogs wandered in and crunched on the bones and fallen food scraps.

Peace fell on the village.

'Tomorrow will be a wonderful day,' Hallbera said as she tucked a cloak round sleepy Magnus on the floor of the hall.

Hilda lay down by the ashes of fire and dozed.

Only Eric stayed awake and thought about the plans he had to make.

'I can do it,' he said. 'If my God helps me, I can do it. I just hope my God is stronger than the Norse gods!' He knelt on the floor, put his hands together and looked up into the clouds of smoke that floated in the lantern light. He prayed.

***

A cruel wind blew over the mountains but Eric was happy. It was still blowing towards England.

The villagers carried heaps of old hay onto Thorfinn's knorr and made a huge bed of it in the cattle pen. This would burn fiercely and turn the passengers to ashes before the ship went down to the Hall of Aegir.

Magnus watched, silent. He was dressed in his bearskin shirt, open at the front, and didn't seem to feel the cold.

Happy Hilda paraded from the great hall to the ship in her green dress and wore a warm woollen cloak of green over the top.

'Why all the hay?' she asked Eric.

He couldn't say: 'So you will burn well,' could he?

'For the sheep,' he answered.

'Of course!' Hilda said, clapping a hand to her forehead. 'I can't go back to England without anything. I have to take the treasure I earned in Norway. They'll be so proud of me on Tyneside when I come home a rich woman. Why, I may even find myself a fine husband.'

'Hmmm!' Eric nodded. 'Are there many blind men on Tyneside?'

But Hilda wasn't listening. 'Why are they putting your boat of life on the knorr?'

'It's a life-boat … and they are putting it on because I will need it.'

'You're coming too?' Hilda said. 'So that's your plan! We sail off in the knorr and you can do the sailing. After all there is blood in your ships on Wearside, isn't there?'

'Ships in my blood, you mean. But, yes, that's my plan.'

'But why take the coracle?' she demanded. 'To get us ashore at the other end of our journey? But the Vikings don't know of your plan … that will give the secret away!'

Eric shook his head. 'Listen, Hilda, I didn't tell you the Viking plan. Not the full plan.'

'They'll send me out with Sigurd … they think I'll chuck him over the side and then sail back?'

'No,' Eric said carefully. 'Not quite … they send you out with Sigurd, they set the ship on fire and you both go to Valhalla together.'

Hilda turned pale. 'You knew that? I've slept the night away when I could have escaped?'

'There's nowhere to run to,' Eric said. 'If you went to the mountains you'd freeze before nightfall. The knorr is the only way out.'

'A burning knorr! Well, thanks you wooden-headed thrall-monk,' she raged. 'I wish I'd never saved your life.'

'Be quiet and listen, will you?' Eric said angrily. 'They can't set the boat adrift and then set it on fire. Because the person who sets it on fire would burn to death.'

'Oh,' Hilda said. 'So?'

'They are putting Magnus on the ship but they don't trust him to do a good job. So I said I would do it. I have the coracle. I said I'd make sure the ship is on fire then escape in my life-boat.'

'Your boat of life? That is brilliant! Instead of setting the knorr on fire you'll sail off to England! That is very clever, thrall-monk. I knew I'd saved your life for a reason! Will it work?'

'Yes,' he said. But Eric knew there were two problems they had to face if they were going to get home safely.

'Oh, look!' she cried. 'They are even putting my sheep aboard! Perfect.'

'Food for Sigurd in Valhalla,' Eric explained.

'Riches for me when I get back to England. My mother won't mind taking me back when I have six sheep to sell!'

The sheep bleated unhappily as they felt the knorr rock beneath them. Sheep like solid ground. 'I hope they won't be ill,' Eric said.

Hilda snorted, 'Hah! They're simply six sea-sick sheep,' she said.

'That's easy for you to say,' the boy told her and began to haul the sail up the mast.

Of course it ISN'T easy for Hilda to say that. It isn't easy for anyone to say 'simply six sea-sick sheep'. Try it and see ... or try it and sea-sick.

The sheep wandered round half of the straw-filled pen. The corpse of Sigurd lay in the other half. The smell of death made the sheep even more restless. The mighty berserker Magnus lay down next to Sigurd. He was armed with a sword and a shield. 'It's off to Valhalla for us, my Lord,' Magnus said. 'It's going to be great being dead, isn't it?' he asked cheerfully.

'No,' Eric said softly.

Magnus was smiling as he lay back and closed his eyes. Soon he was snoring as the boat rocked him like a giant baby's cradle.

SHEEP, SAILS AND A SUNSET

The tide caught the boat as Thorfinn untied his knorr. 'Goodbye, old boat,' he said and wiped a tear from his eye. 'I loved sailing with you. We had some good times together. I'll miss you!'

'What about me?' Hilda raged. She didn't understand every word he said but guessed what he was saying. The wind caught the sail and pushed the boat towards the sea. 'You … miss … me?'

'I can always buy another thrall … maybe next time I'll buy a boy and he won't be so stubborn. With my share of the treasures of Lindisfarne I may even buy two thralls!'

Hilda didn't understand that at all. Eric did.

'It's Lindisfarne,' he said and his stomach jumped into his throat the way grass leaps into the throat of a sea-sick sheep.

'What's Lindisfarne?' Hilda asked.

'The raid. The Viking attack will be on Lindisfarne Monastery … not Jarrow on the Tyne, or Wearmouth Monastery. It's Lindisfarne! How did the Vikings find out about its treasures?'

Hilda shrugged. 'We stopped at a monastery on an island on our last trip … the trip where we saved you. We went ashore to shelter from a storm.'

Eric understood. 'There was a storm … while I was washed out to sea you were driven to shelter on the island.

When the storm died you sailed east and found me. Why didn't you tell me?' Eric groaned.

'I didn't think it was important,' Hilda sniffed. 'I had to stay on the knorr with Freydis because they didn't want women in the monastery. We were battered by the storm for hours. But not Thorfinn!' she raged. 'Oh, no! Because he was a man they took him in to the monastery. They fed him with part of the funeral feast they were having…'

'Funeral!' Eric cried. 'They are my friends! Who died?'

'A boy – a novice,' she shrugged.

'Ethelbert? Don't say it was Ethelbert,' Eric moaned.

Hilda sighed. 'Thorfinn didn't speak the language well. And I don't speak his language well so I don't really know. All I understood was "young monk" and "died" and "feast".'

'I'll find out who it was tomorrow,' Eric said.

'How?'

'Because we are sailing to Lindisfarne. In this leaking barrel we might make it by tomorrow night, I guess.'

'But I want to go home to Jarrow,' Hilda argued. 'And you want to go on to Wearside. You're going to be a boat-builder, you said.'

'We have to warn my friends on Lindisfarne first,' Eric said and hauled the sail to the very top so it caught every breath of the cold east wind and pushed them forward. The wind also carried voices from the shore.

Hilda turned. 'What's wrong with the villagers?'

Eric took the steering oar from her and turned the ship

a little more to the north and west. The villagers were standing by the shore while some of the warriors had climbed into the hills to get a better view.

'They are waiting to see you die,' Eric said. 'They expected me to lower the sail and start the fire, not sail off towards England.'

'They can't stop us now,' Hilda said happily. When the boy didn't reply she asked, 'Can they?'

'Two problems,' he told her as he wrestled with the steering oar to turn the knorr against the swift currents and rolling waves. 'They have their longships. I only sailed one for a short way but I know they have the speed of an eagle – we have the speed of a duck with a broken wing.'

'They'll catch us?'

'Yes ... but the tide is going out fast and their dragon ships are on the beach. I don't think they can sail till the next high tide ... which is tonight. We have half a day's start. We are the slow, fat rabbit and they are the greyhound. They will always win a race ... but we may get to safety before they catch us.'

'So it's a race,' the girl said and looked back at the grey, rocky land they were leaving behind. 'Who will win?'

Eric shook his head slowly. 'Father Patrick told a story…'

'Who's he?'

'The abbot in charge of the monastery … he told us about the slaves of Israel escaping from Egypt. They reached a sea and had to cross it. It was a race.'

'Just like us?'

'Mmm. The sea parted – the people of Israel walked across the dry seabed. When the Egyptians tried to follow, the sea closed in again and drowned them.'

'Can YOU do that for us?' Hilda asked.

'I can ask,' Eric muttered. 'But there's another Bible story we need more … the story of little David who killed Goliath the giant with a sling and a stone.'

He looked at the sleeping form of Magnus the berserker in the middle of the ship. 'He'll wake up sooner or later. That's our second problem.'

'So do you have a sling and a stone like David in the Bible?'

'No,' Eric said.

'So you can't kill him?'

'No.'

'And when he wakes up he will probably kill us.'

'Probably,' Eric admitted.

'So this is your great escape plan?'

'I did say there were two problems,' Eric reminded the girl. 'The dragon ships are one. Magnus is the other.'

Hilda spread her hands. 'Ye-es, I can see how Magnus killing us could be a problem. Didn't you think about that in your plan? Didn't you bring your fish knife with you to slit his throat while he's asleep?'

The young monk shook his head very slowly. 'No, Hilda, I don't think killing is the answer. There must be a better way.'

'What is it then?' she asked.

'Don't know,' he replied.

'Great,' she muttered.

***

The sun was a faint golden ball behind thin grey clouds and it showed it was about noon. Magnus woke at last. He rubbed his eyes and stretched.

'Is this Valhalla then?' he asked.

'No. This is the North Sea,' Eric told him. 'My arms are aching from holding this steering paddle. Come and take it,' he ordered. The captain of a ship is like a lord in his own castle and everyone must obey.

Magnus climbed out of the pen and rolled along towards the stern where he took the paddle from Eric. 'So we're not dead then?'

'No. Sigurd is dead but you, Hilda, me and the sheep are alive.'

Magnus scowled. 'The girl has to die and so do I,' Magnus said. 'Shall I kill her now? Before you set the boat alight? It will be quicker for her.'

Eric looked at the Viking and sat on the deck of the ship. 'Magnus,' he said. 'Those stories about Valhalla…'

'What about them?'

'Well … the Norse believe them, but the English don't.

We have a much nicer place we go to ... a place called Heaven.'

'Is it full of brave warriors?'

'No, it's full of good people.'

As the round ship wallowed and wobbled westwards Eric told Magnus all the stories that Father Patrick had told the young monks at Lindisfarne. Tales of loving your enemy and how kind and forgiving people are the best. Hilda brought them bread and cheese and ale as Eric talked on till it was dark.

At last the young monk lay on the deck and fell asleep.

When he awoke next morning he was covered with Magnus's bearskin shirt. Dawn light was turning the sky a sheepish shade of cream. Hilda was asleep among her sheep for warmth and Magnus was still steering west. Magnus wore just a woollen shirt and didn't seem to feel the cold.

He smiled when he saw Eric open his eyes and waken. 'Why do the Norse people not know about your Bible stories?' he asked the boy.

'Because the people of England don't speak Norse,' Eric told him.

'You do.'

'My mother was a Norse living in England.'

Magnus nodded. 'Then you should go to Norway and tell your stories.'

Eric frowned. 'They would kill me,' he said simply.

'So? They kill you ... you go to your wonderful Heaven! Better than Valhalla!' Magnus said.

'Ye-e-es...' Eric said. 'But not just yet!'

They sailed on all day, taking turns at steering. Eric kept glancing back to see if he could see dragon heads looming over the horizon, racing to catch them before they reached Lindisfarne. Some time in the afternoon they wrapped Sigurd's corpse in his cloak, fastened his sword to his neck and lowered him into the sea.

We may never know if Sigurd went to Valhalla or not. But you can be pretty sure the six sea-sick sheep felt happier. Be honest, you don't like sharing a bed with a dead body that is starting to rot and smell, do you? So why would those six sea-sick sheep on a ship?

Evening began to fall and the sea turned black as a bat's eyeball. As the sun set it broke through the clouds in a blood-red blaze and showed the hills of England ahead. Eric knew the hills and steered the ship a little further north so they would land on Lindisfarne. As he turned to the steering paddle he looked back. The red sun was staining the sea and lighting a square sail just coming over the horizon.

He looked at Hilda. 'We'll win the race ... but only just.'

'We could head south to the Tyne and save ourselves, couldn't we?' she said. 'The Vikings are heading for Lindisfarne.'

Eric didn't give a straight answer to her question. 'At Lindisfarne there are many monks. I'll tell you about two.

Ethelbert is my age. His parents died when he was a baby and the people of his village gave him to the monastery so the monks could care for him. He's never known any other life. He's not like you or me. He's never lived in the outside world. If he's still alive when the Vikings take him they will make him a thrall and send him to work for some hard master.'

Hilda said nothing.

'And then there's Father Patrick. He is as mad as a berserker. But when he tells stories people listen. He is the only teacher I've known but I think he is the best teacher in England. He taught me and I used his teaching to teach Magnus. Father Patrick can be harsh with his rod but his teaching can turn even the Vikings away from their ruthless ways … in time.'

As the words poured out, Eric realised he couldn't remember when he had changed his mind about Father Patrick. In fact, since he'd been living among the vicious Vikings, Eric wasn't even sure why he had run from the monastery in the first place.

Eric tugged a rope and the knorr swung round. Now he could see a silhouette against the sunset that he knew was Lindisfarne.

'When the Vikings arrive they will look at Father Patrick and see just an old man ... too old to be worth anything as a thrall. They will kill him.'

The sheep began to bleat as they smelled the shore. The waves slapped the side of the old ship. A monastery bell began to ring to call the monks to their evening service. At last Hilda spoke quietly. 'We go to Lindisfarne. We save them all.'

Eric shook his head. 'We can't. We aren't Thor and Frey. We're not gods and we can't save the monastery against a hundred murderous Vikings. We can't even save the treasure ... the gold and silver crosses and cups and candlesticks. We can only hope to save the most precious things on the island, Ethelbert and Father Patrick.'

Hilda nodded her head. 'Sometimes you say some wise things for a stupid thrall-boy.'

'I think that's what Father Patrick taught me,' Eric smiled.

'So let's save them!' Hilda laughed.

The shore was rushing towards them. The sun vanished and a dimness fell over the sea. The bells stopped. Even the sheep fell silent.

There was a faint sound of monks chanting.

Then there was a sudden louder sound ... a tearing, grasping, grating, wrenching, splintering, shivering sound.

'We've hit a rock!' Magnus cried from the front of the ship.

'Ship-wrecked again!' Hilda cried. 'We can't get Magnus and the sheep in the boat of life,' she cried.

Water was starting to bubble in through the cracked seams at the front of the knorr. In the dim light of a rising moon the boy and girl saw Magnus throw himself over the front of the boat. 'Are you walking on water?' Eric cried.

'No, I'm standing on the rock we're wrecked on,' Magnus grunted. 'I'm like Fjalar and Galar on a rock in the sea!'

'They drowned,' Eric reminded him.

'Yes, but only when the tide came in. The giant was saved,' Magnus said.

'We're not giants!' Eric said as he staggered to keep standing in the tilting boat.

'I am,' Magnus said. 'The girl first!'

'What's happening?' Hilda asked.

'Magnus will carry you ashore,' Eric explained.

'I'm not leaving my sheep,' the girl argued.

'He'll carry you ashore and come back for your sheep,' Eric cried. 'But hurry!'

Magnus scooped Hilda under one mighty arm and a sheep under the other. On the next two journeys he carried two sheep each time. When Magnus had lifted the last sheep to safety, Eric paddled ashore in his coracle and joined them.

He was just in time. The tide was rising and swallowing the knorr that was stuck fast on the rock. At last they were all standing on the narrow beach of Lindisfarne; the same beach that Eric had been blown from just two weeks before.

'Hilda ... take the sheep along this path ... keep the monastery to your right and go straight ahead. Cross to the mainland.'

'This is an island!' she said. 'I can't swim and neither can my sheep.'

'There is a path of sand ... they call it the causeway ... across the water when the tide is low. It runs from the island to the mainland of Northumbria. If you get there quickly you'll make it. Go, now!' he shouted over the noise of the waves crashing over the pebbled beach. 'Wait for us on the other side. If we don't get across before the tide covers the causeway then go on south without us.'

Hilda gathered her sheep and started to drive them ahead of her. They seemed happy to be back on land. 'I'll pray for you,' she promised as she disappeared into the shadows of the monastery.

Magnus picked up the coracle and the two marched to the open gate of the monastery.

'Leave the coracle by the sea gate,' Eric said, pointing to a small door in the monastery wall, and Magnus obeyed.

Lantern-light spilled out from the church and the crisp air carried the voices of the monks.

Eric stepped through the door. He saw rows of kneeling hooded monks turned towards the altar of silver and gold. Only Father Patrick, standing at the altar, was facing him. He looked up. He saw Eric. He clutched at a silver candlestick to stop himself falling.

'Lord save us,' he said in his soft voice. 'It's a ghost!'

The monks all turned to see Eric standing there. They fell to their knees, fumbling with their crosses. Only Father Patrick stayed on his feet and Ethelbert, who walked towards his friend. 'We had your funeral two weeks ago, Eric. You're dead!'

MOONLIGHT, MONASTERIES AND A MOTHER

Eric gripped his friend by the arms and shook him. 'I'm not dead, Ethelbert.'

'Father Patrick said we had to pray for you or you'd go to Hell. Did you go to Hell?' Ethelbert frowned.

Eric moaned, 'I haven't time to tell you now…'

'What's it like in Hell?'

'I met a really ugly girl and she sold me as a thrall and I had to steal a ship to get home.'

'It sounds an awful place!'

'It was Hell,' Eric agreed. 'Now this is Magnus – he doesn't speak English but trust me, he's a good Norseman. Go with him.'

Father Patrick had walked over to the door and was frowning at Eric. 'You are not a devil and you didn't die?'

'No, but some devils are on the way … they call themselves Vikings – pirates – and they'll be here very soon. We have to flee to the mainland. Let them have the silver and gold, but save yourself!'

Father Patrick shook his head and said, 'My place is here with my brothers.'

The east wind carried Norse cheers of joy as the Viking invaders began to jump from their ships, their long journey over. They would see the light in the church. They would race over the turf with the greed for gold driving their legs. They would swing their silver swords in the golden lights to cut through anyone in their way.

Eric wanted to explain. He didn't have time. He turned to Magnus and spoke quickly in Norse. 'This man is a berserker,' he said nodding at Father Patrick. 'You were cured of your madness with a blow to the head. Save him now. Strike his head … but don't kill him!'

Magnus nodded and moved behind Father Patrick.

'What were you saying?' Father Patrick demanded. 'Were you speaking in the tongue of the Devil? Were you…'

Clunk!

Father Patrick's eyes went dead as a snuffed candle and he slowly toppled forward. Magnus scooped him under his arm before he hit the ground. 'Make for the causeway!' he ordered Magnus in Norse. 'Ethelbert!' he went on in English, 'Show him the way across the causeway and go with him.'

'And you?'

'I'll follow. Go!'

'The tide is coming in,' Ethelbert argued. 'You know the tides, Eric. We might make it. But you won't if you don't leave now!'

'Go!' shouted Eric.

Ethelbert shrugged unhappily and took Magnus by the sleeve to show the way through the gloom. They had soon vanished through the monastery gates with the lifeless bundle of Father Patrick under Magnus's arm.

The monks were trembling and unable to believe what they'd just seen.

The Viking voices were growing louder. Every moment put Eric's life more at risk. 'Brothers there are devils coming. You cannot stop them. They are starving and desperate men. All you can do is run and save yourselves. If you leave now you may catch the causeway. If you stay you could die.'

The monks looked at one another, baffled and unhappy. 'Ohhh!' Eric wailed as he saw them staying on their knees. He turned and ran.

The Viking Helgi the Sly was rounding the corner of the church and saw Eric racing away. As the other Vikings turned into the church Helgi paused. 'Look for the gold!' he ordered his men.

The Vikings poured over the churchyard and trampled the graves of the monks who were long dead and dusty.

Eric heard the cries of terror from the monks and the roars of rage from the invaders. As he passed the gateway he snatched up his coracle and hurried after the others.

A roar from behind him showed the faint shape of the Viking warrior racing down the slope towards him. Helgi the Sly had come after him.

Helgi was fast and he didn't have a coracle to weigh him down. The sea was twenty paces to Eric's left ... the causeway was two hundred paces ahead of him. He would never make the causeway.

As Helgi the Sly's feet pounded over the turf, every step brought him closer to his prey. Eric threw himself to the left and Helgi skidded as he tried to stop. Eric tumbled over the pebbles and threw the coracle into the water. He jumped after it and looked back to see the Viking wading in to snatch at the coracle and catch him.

Eric's paddle flew like a butterfly wing and he slipped away as Helgi's fingernails scraped at the edge of the little boat, before he had to let go.

Helgi roared then looked across the moonlit water. He saw Magnus walking across the causeway two hundred paces to his right. The berserker had one old monk under his arm and a young one riding on his back.

Eric watched helpless from the safety of the sea as Helgi waded back to shore and ran after Magnus. Magnus was a mighty man but he had no sword or shield. Not even Magnus could survive the cold, sharp iron of a slicing Viking sword.

There was sea to the left of the path and sea to the right. Eric paddled hard till he reached the sea to the left and watched as Helgi stepped onto the sand.

'The children of Israel fled over a break in the sea like this!' Eric cried in Norse.

Helgi stopped and looked at him. 'Who?'

'The people that God chose,' Eric told him and let the coracle drift nearer. 'God let them get across. He saved them. When their enemies stepped onto the path the waters rose. It was a miracle.'

Helgi jumped off the sandy path to try and catch Eric in the shallow water. Eric let him get near enough to smell his body then paddled away. Helgi snarled and turned back to where the causeway had been. In the dim light of a half-moon he searched for the path. It had vanished. The tide had risen just enough to cover it.

At the far end of the causeway, near the mainland Magnus was splashing through the shallow but rising water. He was simply walking straight and he had Ethelbert to guide him. Helgi could have run across the shallow water and caught them … but he couldn't see the path in the silver light and was confused by Eric's words. The Viking looked back at the island of Lindisfarne and began to struggle back to the monastery. There were deep pools that sucked at his legs and rocks below the water that tripped him. At last he reached the shore and looked back. Eric had vanished and Magnus was in the shadows of the far shore with his burden of monks.

Helgi the Sly splashed back to the monastery to make sure of his share of the gold and thralls.

It was to be a bitter and pitiless night on Lindisfarne.

The sun rose on the smoking ruins of the fine church, stripped of every ounce of precious metal. It rose on the cheerless moans of monks as they were tied and thrown aboard the dragon ships to face a life of slavery.

But at least they had a life. The Vikings left behind those monks who'd tried to flee and had been cruelly cut down. They left them scattered in the churchyard, unburied.

Lindisfarne was left to the sad wail of the wind in the ruins and the cries of the gulls over the icy sea.

The dragon prows were turned towards Norway. The Viking leader, Helgi the Sly, looked at his loot and took one last glance back. He gave a savage smile. 'Thank you, England, we'll be back. Oh, yes, we'll be back!'

And the world had changed forever.

***

The rest of the story is quickly told.

Hilda led the group of escapees south till they reached the River Tyne. They crossed it at the old Roman bridge and headed east to Jarrow.

She went home and showed her six sheep to her mother to the wonder of the poor woman. 'You won't send me away again, mother, will you?'

'Not a rich girl like you, Hilda. Now who are your friends? They look nice.' She served Magnus and Eric, Ethelbert and Father Patrick with the best food Jarrow could find. After all, she was rich now. As she stirred the pot of mutton stew over the fire she nudged her daughter in the ribs. She nodded at Eric. 'That Eric, the one with the fair hair … he's handsome! Have you found yourself a husband?'

Hilda threw her eyes up to the January skies. 'Mother! He's from Wearside!'

'Really! Poor boy … and I thought he looked such a nice young man. What about the weedy one in the brown robe?'

'He's a monk. Monks don't marry.'

'What about the monster of a man. He really is gorgeous – clean the food out of his beard, give him a bath and he'll make a fine husband!'

'What? Mad Magnus? No, mother. Not my type.'

Her mother gave a smile through the smoke. 'He might be my type though!'

'He doesn't speak English.' Hilda told her mother.

'I'll teach him. We need a strong man around the house. He can work for his keep. Oh, yes … a nice strong man!'

'Mother … you … you're…'

'What?'

Hilda sighed. She couldn't put it into words. But her mother made her blush and wish the roof would fall on her head and hide her.

Warning. The words Hilda was looking for were, 'Mother, you are showing me up.' But, of course, that is what parents do. Show up their children. It is their job, as you know. You get to the age of 5 and you suddenly discover that parents embarrass you. Here's the BAD news … you get to 55 and they are STILL doing it.

So Magnus stayed in Jarrow. His skill as a warrior was worth more than gold and silver. 'This is how the Vikings fight,' he told the men of Tyneside. 'And this is how you can stop them!'

The time when they would need his skills was closer than they realised...

The Jarrow monks welcomed Father Patrick and Ethelbert and wrote their gory story of the attack on Lindisfarne. It was sent around the country as a warning to their brothers everywhere.

Eric parted from Hilda as friendly as ever. 'My mother is pleased to have me back,' the girl said.

Eric smiled, 'I'm sure she is. Of course she doesn't know you would sell her as a thrall if someone offered you half a sheep. Goodbye, Hilda.'

She answered him in the way little Harald back in Norway would have done. She placed her tongue between her lips and blew. 'Pttthhhht!'

Eric went eight miles south to Wearside and showed the men there how to build longships. And so he should have stayed there till he died ... but...

One autumn day, eight months after his escape from Lindisfarne, as he was planing planks, he looked up from his work. A tall young monk stood and grinned at him. 'Ethelbert? Is that you? You've grown so much I hardly recognised you! You've come to see your brothers at Wearmouth monastery?'

'No. I've come to see you,' Ethelbert said. And he told his tale.

'Father Patrick is dying. Before he dies he has one last

132

dream. He wants peace. He thinks that if the Vikings learn about our God – instead of their vicious fighting gods like Thor – we may all be able to live in peace together.'

Eric smiled. 'It worked with Magnus,' he said.

'Because you were the monk that talked to him. Father Patrick thinks you are the only person that can save England. He will tell you all he knows before he dies. Come back with me and be a monk again.'

'But I'm a ship builder!' Eric objected.

'Ships can never sail in peace while the vicious Vikings are out there in their dragon boats,' Ethelbert said.

Eric handed his plane over to one of the other workers, and threw a woollen coat over his working clothes.

'You'll do it?' Ethelbert grinned. 'You'll come back with me?'

'Building boats is hard work ... but saving England? With your help, of course ... that's easy!'

'It's dangerous,' Ethelbert said quietly. 'If the Norse don't like your stories they will kill you. What was it that your mother told you?'

'She said that I should never be afraid. The gods will decide when I am going to die — I could wear all the armour in the world but if I am doomed then I will die.'

'Then we live or die together,' Ethelbert said.

Eric wrapped an arm around Ethelbert's shoulder and together the two friends walked off into the sunset.

ENDINGS AND BEGINNINGS

The rest of the tale you can read in the history books. A monk wrote the famous diary that started this story...

'In this year fierce, frightening signs were seen in the heavens over Northumbria. There were mighty whirlwinds, lightning storms, and fiery dragons were seen flying in the sky. These signs were followed by great famine, and on January 8th of the same year, the raging heathen men destroyed God's church at Lindisfarne.'

The heathen men were the Vikings. The year was 793 AD. The Norsemen wrecked Lindisfarne, stole its treasures then sailed back home.

Of course some monks said the Viking attacks served the English people right. It was a punishment for being wicked. A monk called Alcuin wrote...

'Think, brothers, maybe this curse arrived because of your evil ways. Look at the rich clothes, the proud way they wear their hair, the rich feasts of the princes and people.'

Yes, the awful Alcuin blamed haircuts for the Viking attacks! Some schools make pupils have neat hair. But even the worst headteacher in the world doesn't say, 'Get your hair cut or big men with swords will drive you into the sea, make you slaves or hack your head off!' Alcuin SHOULD have said, 'Get your hair cut because it helps to get rid of the nits.'

But someone must have escaped that Lindisfarne raid. A monk survived to tell the terrible tale about the Viking attack – and how the monastery was wrecked. Some monks were driven into the sea, some were made thralls and some were simply killed.

The Vikings went back to Norway with their treasure and thought, 'That was easy! Let's do it again next year!'

But Lindisfarne had been robbed something rotten. The greedy Vikings had to try another monastery in another place. So, the next year, they came back and attacked Jarrow Monastery on Hilda's Tyneside and Wearmouth on Eric's Wearside.

This was a massive mistake. The people of Tyneside were waiting. They captured the Viking chief. The Vikings asked, 'Can we have him back, please?'

The people of Tyneside sent him back ... in a box ... chopped into pieces.

WHO could have warned the folk of Jarrow and Wearside? Could it have been a rather plain-looking girl and a half-blood Norse boy? Who knows.

Who taught those Tynesiders how to fight? A berserker

who forgot how to be angry? Perhaps.

But year after year the Vikings came back. In time they brought their wives and families and they came to stay. The English were driven back to the south and west of Britain while the Vikings settled in the north.

It was the famous King Alfred the Great who finally saved the English. But what helped was that the Vikings gave up their old religion. Someone taught them the English way. Some monk, probably. Some young monk who knew the Viking language?

We don't know. But it's a good guess.

The Vikings still kept thralls ... but at least they stopped stabbing, hanging, drowning and breaking their backs as sacrifices to the Old Norse gods.

Some Vikings even ate some of their human sacrifices. Imagine being a cannibal and eating your victim. I suppose you could always mash their eyeballs with frozen milk to make eyes-cream. They also sacrificed dogs and horses. Aren't you pleased you're not an old Viking?

By the 900s some Vikings moved to France and the French Vikings became even nastier Norsemen ... but their name changed to 'Normans'.

When the Normans attacked England in 1066 they smashed the Saxons and stayed to rule over the whole country. So, in a way, the Vikings won in the end.

And what of Eric's Wearmouth? Its name became Sunderland and in time it became the greatest shipbuilding town in the world.

Eric would have been very happy to know that.

If you enjoyed Raiders and
Ruins, then you'll love
four more Gory Stories,
written by Terry Deary.
Why not read the
whole horrible lot?

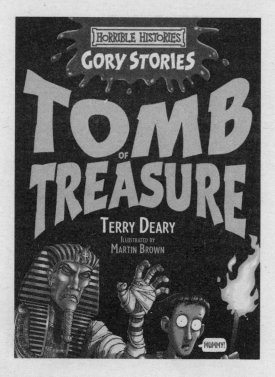

Phoul Pharaoh Tutankhamun has died and is about to be buried. It's master-thief Antef's big moment – can he and his crew of criminals pull off the biggest grave-robbery of all time and empty Tut's tomb of its richest treasures?

Find out in this Awful Egyptian adventure, it's got all the gore and so much more!

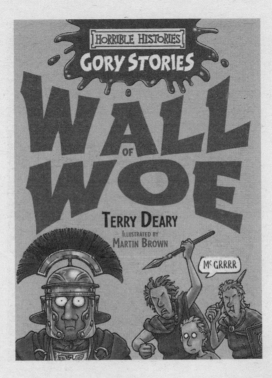

A wild and wind-lashed wall separates two terrifying tribes: the Picts and the Britons. Two Gaul soldiers are given the task of guarding the wall – on pain of death. But with catapults, feasts and football to distract them, will they be able to keep the peace and solve the mystery of the lost legion?

Find out in this Rotten Roman adventure, it's got all the gore and so much more!

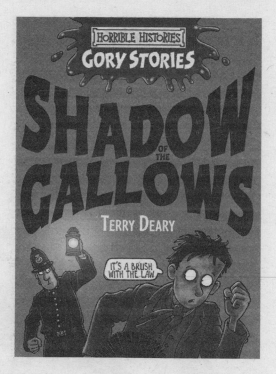

When a boy called Bairn is rescued from his dangerous job as an Edinburgh chimney sweep, he appears to have landed on his feet. But his new job proves just as dangerous and he soon becomes caught up in a plot to kill Queen Victoria. Has he been saved from slavery only to end up swinging at the gallows?

Find out in this Vile Victorian adventure, it's got all the gore and so much more!

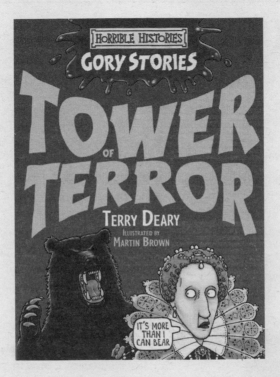

Simon Tuttle and his Pa are tricksters struggling to make a living on the Tudor streets. When disaster strikes Simon must fend for himself, even if it means committing treason. But can he pull off his Pa's carefully concocted plan and should he trust his mysterious new accomplice?

Find out in this Terrible Tudor adventure, it's got all the gore and so much more!

Terry Deary was born at a very early age, so long ago he can't remember. But his mother, who was there at the time, says he was born in Sunderland, north-east England, in 1946 – so it's not true that he writes all *Horrible Histories* from memory. At school he was a horrible child only interested in playing football and giving teachers a hard time. His history lessons were so boring and so badly taught, that he learned to loathe the subject. *Horrible Histories* is his revenge.

Martin Brown was born in Melbourne, on the proper side of the world. Ever since he can remember he's been drawing. His dad used to bring back huge sheets of paper from work and Martin would fill them with doodles and little figures. Then, quite suddenly, with food and water, he grew up, moved to the UK and found work doing what he's always wanted to do: drawing doodles and little figures.